The Next Hedgerow
A Correspondence

Copyright © 2004 Peter Rutkoff
All rights reserved
Printed in USA
ISBN 1-880977-10-9

First edition, second printing
August 2006

Book design by Jerry Kelly
Cover design by Rebecca Taylor
Cover painting "Jacket" courtesy of the artist
Karen Snouffer, from her series "Verdant Years"
Cover painting photograph by Ed Schiebel
Printed by Printing Arts Press, Mt. Vernon, OH

Harry Rutkoff (b. 1910—d. 1949)
Peter Rutkoff (b. 1942)

PRESS
GAMBIER, OHIO

see us at www.xoxoxpress.com
write us at books@xoxoxpress.com

The Next Hedgerow
A Correspondence

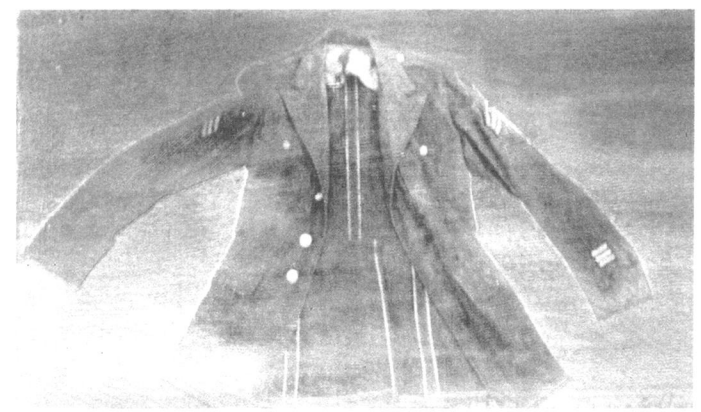

Harry Rutkoff
&
Peter Rutkoff

XOXOX PRESS

VETERANS ADMINISTRATION
REGIONAL OFFICE
252 SEVENTH AVENUE
NEW YORK 1, NEW YORK

Office of
CHIEF ATTORNEY

Oct. 2, 1959

YOUR FILE REFERENCE:

IN REPLY REFER TO: 3006:272D

Mr. Peter Rutkoff
20 W. 84-th Street
New York, N.Y.

XC 3 962 501
RUTKOFF, Harry

Peter Rutkoff (minor)

Dear Mr. Rutkoff:

This will certify that according to our records, your father, Harry Rutkoff, served in the United States Army from November 22, 1943, until his honorable discharge on January 17, 1946. His serial number was: 42 052 120 and his death on December 16, 1949 was the result of this military service.

Very truly yours,

Frank Klipper

FRANK KLIPPER
Acting Chief Attorney

This letter allowed me to use my father's V.A. benefits to pay for my undergraduate college education. P.R.

An inquiry by or concerning an ex-service man or woman should, if possible, give veteran's name and file number, whether C, XC, K, N, V, H, RH, RS, W, or loan number. If such number is unknown, service or serial number should be given.

THE NEXT HEDGEROW:
A CORRESPONDENCE

INTRODUCTION
by Peter Rutkoff
6

THREE STORIES AND A POEM
by Harry Rutkoff
9

Way of Life
Nightshirt in the Ardennes
Freedom
Poem

V-MAILS AND LETTERS,
MAY-SEPTEMBER, 1944
by Harry Rutkoff
36

STORY
by Peter Rutkoff
55

Deux Marc

ABOUT THE AUTHORS
80

INTRODUCTION

My father rarely had the opportunity to speak to me. Later, after he died, they told me how eloquent and playful his language could be. But, then, in the years after the War he walked around our house in silence. Or, so I recall. I think, now, of our lives as overlapping-like two pages in a book-for such a brief time—his, transparent, overlay across mine. He was home, bum leg, as he called it, cane, pipes and humidor, shaving cream, and a scar that claimed his entire right shoulder. I can't remember any conversations, only his footfalls and smells. I can't hear his voice. Did he have an accent, or repeat a favorite phrase? It's as if I have been struck deaf in his presence, that sense denied.

He died, my father, when I was seven and he thirty-nine. It took five years from the time he was wounded, terribly wounded, in the fields of France, in the fierce hedgerow fighting, till the dark winter night they told me that he had died. And after they told me, after my mother held me and I screamed, the world was completely silent. Silent, I mean, in the sense of a deafening noiselessness, at that very moment. First my mother's voice, then an explosion of silence filling my ears.

I realize now that my father left me only snapshots-an image here and there-of driving the car or eating breakfast. But these images have neither motion nor sound, only silence.

Even as his generation falls ill and dies, they manage to leave their voices, I have noticed, on their answering machines. Their accents are the fingerprints of identity that keep their memory alive. My father's best friend, Charles Rutkoff, was also his first cousin and my substitute parent. Charlie is 93 now and he can no longer recognize me. But his voice is still on the tape. And when I call his wife, Sylvia, who has been a mother to me all these years, his voice echoes back to me over half a century. I can hear Charlie still, in his manhood, through that voice. "Peter my lad," he loved to say before delivering his wisdom. "Peter my lad, in my day…"

And it was dear Charlie who one day sent me a package of "stuff your father asked me to keep for you." A brown, brittle cardboard folder, marled and scarred, opened to reveal a packet of onion skin paper. There it was, three stories and a poem, all written by Harry Rutkoff, 425 Riverside Drive, New York, N.Y. My father, his legacy lying asleep on a dusty shelf in an attic in New Jersey—now in my hands, his voice.

It was as if some cosmic door had opened, for a few months later I visited my Aunt Anne, my father's sister, like Charlie, now 93. She sounds like the west Bronx, somehow both working class and cultured, and she asks, would I like my father's letters? She hands me a bundle of V-Mail, from England, from France, from the battle field, from the hospital, from the hedgerows. Letters that her brother Harry wrote to the family, to her, to her parents, to my mother and to me. "Chuck Peter on the head," he wrote in one. There, we were together, I marveled. I could almost hear his voice.

Together these stories, the poem, and his letters have allowed Harry Rutkoff to speak. They speak to me, my children, the grandchildren he never knew, and now to his first readers, more than fifty years after his death. It is as if the little boy I once was, peeping out from behind his blanket in the hallway, finally can turn on the sound.

Peter Rutkoff
Gambier, Ohio
August, 2004

Harry Rutkoff: Stories

Harry, 1942

Way of Life

"Ya don' say nothin'," Vic said, "An' ya don' pull no double guard duty jist when the ol' horseshoe lands us in a rest area."

"Aw, blow it out," Sal said, "I ain't takin' no bull from a boy scout looey whose been around for two days. Two days! Not me I ain't—after all the combat crap for a month straight. Bull buddy, you ain't been around this guffin' Normandy long enough to know the score."

Sal slapped his web belt, loaded down with clips of .30 calibers around his bulky waist, banged his mud-caked helmet down on his head at an angle, and with tight fingers pulled his rifle out of the folds of his raincoat which was lying in his fox-hole.

His dark, thick-browed face was set hard. Weeks of combat and exposure had worked the mud and grime of battlefields into it and had pinched it until the flesh was tautly pegged down. The sides of his broad nose sloped down into hollows. The lines of his lips had almost disappeared. His brown eyes, almost round normally, were elongated and slitted with weariness.

"Bull," he said, "You got a lot to learn, hillbilly."

"Yep, I guess," Vic sighed, stretching his long thin body wearily in his foxhole, "I wus jist thinkin' to help a buddy."

Buddy, buddy, Sal thought, as he plodded towards his guard post. That stuff. That Vic ain't gonna buddy me. I'll be draggin' his can for him all over the guffin' place. Then he'll get knocked off like the other dumb bastards anyhow. Aw, what the hell can I do? I got my own can to worry about. The guy's got advice for me.

Head-down, heavy footed and stooped, his rifle slung muzzle up on his left shoulder, he moved wearily along the edge of the field. Soldiers were lying at regular intervals in foxholes next to the hedgerow. Most of them were asleep in the shade. A few were putting up pup-tents over their holes, to enjoy the luxury of cover in case of rain even though the summer sun was brilliant and the sky deep blue.

Sal reached the guard post—a weather-beaten gray rail gate at the end of the field near the road. He exchanged nods with the sleepy G.I. he was relieving.

"Ma-reedi-somethin'," he said, giving what he could remember of the password.

"Soup-natchil," the little G.I. returned, then shuffled off.

Sal shoved a clip of .30 calibers into his rifle breech and grounded the piece at his side. Guard. Sonafabitch—what was there to guard? They were miles from the front. Guffin' army. Just to make a guy miserable. They don't give a guff about nothin'—not even a guy's life. You get killed. So what? They bring up a replacement. They got lots of replacements. They just throw you away when you're dead, like the silk thread waste he used to throw into the containers next to the machine in the plant. You never thought about it. Plenty of silk thread around. He sighed. A few days rest. Rest, they call it. And then combat again. What the hell did they do it for—take a man with two kids and a wife and throw him into the army? Sure, Lena'd get along swell on his army insurance and her widow's pension. He took a deep breathe and tensed his shoulder muscles, crinkling his face. Grunting, he let his breath out. He'd have to lick them all—the army, the officers, these damn buddy-buddy G.I.s and the Jerries. There's gotta be a way. There always is, if you're smart enough and got guts.

Yeah, smart enough for that now platoon looey—Merrington. What a name—Merrington! Why could he pronounce it so aptly when the Looey couldn't say "Maniscelloni." Maniscelloni is easy. Anybody who wants to can say it right. Anybody but that lousy boy scout. He shifted his rifle to his other side, bringing the butt-end down hard as he recalled the incident that had gotten him double guard duty. Double guard duty for a combat soldier in a rest area.

He had been standing on the chow-line that morning in the tree shaded sunken road behind the field, blinking his eyes, trying to get used to the quiet. He had been hardly thinking at all, just pleasurably sensing his body's juices welling up when somebody had roughly tried to propel him forward. He had spun around, almost off balance, to find himself facing Lieutenant Merrington, the new platoon commander.

"Move along, soldier," the Lieutenant said. "Men behind you are waiting. Look alive."

Sal stared into his face, tilting his head back a little because the Lieutenant was tall and thin like an upright greyhound. His young face was small featured and almost feminine in the delicacy of its lines.

The Lieutenant, hooking his thumbs onto his belt and leaning back, looked hard at him, waiting.

Sal stood motionless.

The Lieutenant suddenly raised a slender hand, pointed past Sal's ear, and speaking out of the side of his mouth., his thin almost invisible brows knitting under his helmet, said, "I'm ordering you to move on soldier."

"Yeah, I'm goin', Lieutenant," Sal said. "I'm goin'."

Turning, he moved slowly down the chow-line. When he halted, he left a space between himself and the sweating G.I. ahead.

"I obey orders, Lieutenant. Always obey," he said, half-smiling. The G.I.s on the line, watching, smiled too. Quickly the Lieutenant bounded over to him.

"Goddammit, what's your name, rank and serial number, soldier?" he said.

Sal stopped smiling.

"What?"

"I said what's your name, rank and serial number. Hurry up."

"Maniscelloni, Salvatore, PeeEffSee, 347,520,41."

"Listen Manilesconi—"

Sal turned full face to the Lieutenant.

"That ain't the way its pronounced, Lieutenant—it's Man-is-celloni. Easy once you say it right."

"I don't give a goddam how you say it, I—"

"Yeah? Well I do. I don't like people not saying my name right."

The Lieutenant's head trembled a little. After a pause he said in a loud clear voice, "You're assigned to guard duty for this afternoon."

"You do that, Lieutenant, its against the A.R.'s," Sal said.

"Listen," the Lieutenant said., "Listen, soldier, I'm doubling the guard duty. Got anything else to say?"

Sal said nothing. His tight hand imperceptibly pressed his mess gear into his thigh. It tinkled almost inaudibly.

From the rear of the chow-line anonymous G.I.'s shouted, "Let's move. Let's go. Who's holding us up," as if they were unaware of an officer's presence.

Lieutenant Merrington flushed. Suddenly he turned and pounded off to the cook tent.

That was how it had ended. Yeah, he'd have to watch out for that Lieutenant.

In the evening, a couple of hours before sunset, the Platoon Sergeant Gaston came looking for Sal, who was asleep after his four hours standing guard.

He woke him up by pumping his right leg up and down vigorously.

"Hey, what's up," Sal said, "We leavin'? Rest over? Geez! What the hell, whaddyawant wise guy?"

"C'mon shake your can," Gaston said, "G'wan and get the platoon's mail. You're the mailman to-night, to-night. My aching back."

"Geez! Can't a guy get a rest. Rest they call it. Christ, first guard, now the mail. Where the hell's Jansen, He always gets it."

"Dunno. Got a detail. New looey keeps everybody busy. Eager beaver."

"Why me for the mail? G'wan pick on somebody else that ain't had guard duty."

"Can't help it. Looey says you."

Sal buckled on his belt and slung his rifle on his shoulder.

"Oh, the Looey?"

"Yeah!"

So he was on the Lieutenant's list. That was just dandy. Well, the Lieutenant was on his list too.

It was two miles round trip for the mail. He got the mail after an half hour's wait. He riffled thru the letters, found three for himself and shoved them into the pocket of his combat jacket. Then he riffled thru some more and found the Lieutenant's. There were two. One was lavender with a girl's name in the corner and under it a college address. The other was a heavy white bond. On the back it said Merrington Associates Real Estate, Salisbury, Pa. Sure, he thought, he has to work for a livin'. Sure, this little love note's from his poor sufferin' woman. He had an impulse to tear the letters up. But his respect for the sanctity of mail restrained him.

When he got back he turned the letters over to Gaston. Then he shuffled back to his hole and read his own.

Just as darkness fell, orders came to prepare for movement. Sal knew that meant returning to combat. Sighing, he made up his pack, checked his rifle and arranged his equipment. He could hear Vic struggling with his stuff, half-cursing and half-sobbing.

"Aw hell, ya dumb jerk," he said coming to Vic's hold, "Can't you roll that pack yet? Jesus, look. This is how … Keep the safety down on your Em One until we get on the line … Here, lemme load this crap on your back … That'll hold it. Hook it down."

The order came through to move to the trucks. Sal pushed Vic forward to steady him and then shuffled away. Guff him. Let someone else worry about him, he thought. He's gonna get killed. Me too, if I keep nursin' him in combat. He'd have to avoid Vic as much as possible.

The men gathered silently in the dark, under the whip-lash orders of their non-coms—each platoon near its assigned truck. Sal leaned on his rifle. He sighed, fighting to breathe under the pressure of the thought of combat. He could hear other men sighing.

Soon there would be the stench of decomposing men and cattle. Soon he would be cringing at the faintest sound of a plane motor and jerking his head to one side at the hiss of artillery shells passing overhead.

"Maniscelloni?"

"Yeah?" he answered, stiffening at the sound of the Lieutenant's voice.

"C'mere."

Wondering, he came to where the Lieutenant stood near the truck's cab.

"Get my luggage down there," he said, pointing. "And load it in the cab."

Sal stopped dead in his tracks and spat out of the side of his mouth. Then he turned around, lips pursed, and walked back to the rear of the truck.

The Lieutenant rushed after him.

"What the hell's the matter with you? Don't you understand me?"

The men in the platoon gathered around them—watching, listening.

"Yeah. I understand you. I understand English even if my name is Maniscelloni. I went to school," Sal spat again.

"Get that luggage." The Lieutenant extended his arm and shot his hand out in a swift pointing gesture.

Sal stood silent and motionless.

"I ain't your servant., Lieutenant," he said slowly. "I got my own load on my back."

"You're disobeying my order?" the Lieutenant said. His hand was still raised in the pointing gesture. For the first time he looked around at the other men. He lowered his arm, shifting his feet.

"Everybody on the truck," he said, "Everybody."

The men scrambled aboard in a confused melee of packs and rifles. Sal was the last aboard.

"If we weren't on our way to combat I'd have you court-martialed, Manescelloni. Next rest we get I'll deal with you."

"If you live that long."

There was a long silence.

"Is that a threat?"

"Men get killed at the front, Lieutenant."

The Lieutenant looked down at his boots, then up at Manescelloni. Then he strode off and got into the cab of the truck.

"Boy, you told him," someone whispered in the truck.

"Yeah," Sal said. He was thinking, you gotta fight them all. Nobody cares about your wife and kids but yourself.

The trucks began to move into the dark.

By morning the men were in their positions at the front. Sal lay on his back in his freshly dug hole, in a ditch up against a hedgerow. Although he was wearing a heavy woolen undershirt under a woolen shirt and a combat jacket over that, he shivered in the cold dawn as his blood cooled after the exertion of digging. The sun was coming up behind the strangely twisted and polled trees that lined the opposite hedgerow. Soon it would be hot and bright. He'd begin to sweat. Then combat. Better not to think of it. Think, should he eat one of his rations now or not. Should he deepen his hole, or would that be a waste of time? Which? They might move on soon. Nothing was happening here. No artillery. No small arms. No planes. Just silence. A befouled silence. Better eat. He opened a can of meat and beans and began shoveling its cold contents into his mouth with his chow-spoon.

Sergeant Gaston approached.

"Shave!" he said.

"Shave?" Sal stopped eating. "What the hell for? Cat house around?"

"Yeah. Lieutenant says shave right away."

"What?"

"Goin' on a morning patrol. Gotta find Jerry. Maybe at the next hedgerow playing. Maybe one after, or after—all the way to Paris. Gotta look right to meet Jerry. Platoon C.P. in five minutes."

"Mother guffer!"

Sal crammed some more meat and beans into his mouth, then threw the can away.

Cursing, he carefully poured some water out of his water bottle into his helmet and shaved. Then he gathered his equipment and shuffled off to the Platoon C.P.

Looking over the heads of the men, the Lieutenant explained the patrol. It was simple. Where was Jerry? He had pulled back during the night. They were going out to find him. Traps, someone said. Don't worry, the Lieutenant said, he knew all about traps. Everybody on the ball and alert. Keep your eyes open. He'd take care of the traps. Just go forward and keep going.

"Maniscelloni!" The Lieutenant looked at him.

"Yeah?"

"You scout."

Sal held the Lieutenant's unblinking eyes.

"I like getaway man, Lieutenant," he said.

"I said you scout."

Sal shrugged. Nobody ever saves himself by being scared.

"Okay."

The Lieutenant looked away.

"All right lets go. Manescelloni first. Then Gaston. I'll follow. The rest in file behind. Janse—you look fast. You're getaway man. Let's move."

Sal clambered over the hedgerow through an opening in the thick growth and slid down the other side. Quickly he dropped into the drainage ditch along the side hedgerow. Crouching, he went forward, his rifle at the ready. He could hear the other men drop down behind him. As he advanced step by step he scanned the hedgerow across the end of the field. Alternately he held one corner, then the other with his eyes, for minutes at a time, searching for any slight movement that might reveal hidden machine guns. His heart pounded. His face grew hot. Sweat poured down his back and legs. As he drew closer to the hedgerow he could scarcely breathe. He had to force his legs to move. He glanced back past Gaston. The getaway man was beyond the halfway mark. If the Jerries were behind this hedgerow they'd open up now. Hurling himself forward, he raced the remaining short distance to the hedgerow. Breathless, he threw himself flat against it, his head below the level of the top. While the rest of the patrol came up Sal listened. No sounds from the enemy side. Gaston, panting, pulled the pin out of a hand grenade and flipped it over the hedgerow through an opening. Sal pressed his mouth into the earth of the hedgerow as the explosion clawed through his brain and then died away. Still no sounds. They might still be there, having stayed clear of the opening.

Gaston nudged Sal and pointed to the Lieutenant. The Lieutenant motioned to him to go over the hedgerow.

Sal grunted, "Mother guffer."

Then he dragged himself slowly over the hedgerow. Twigs and branches crackled under him. He looked and let out his breath. No one was there. He slid heavily into another side ditch and called softly to the patrol.

With the patrol following he began going down the second ditch. Great outbursts of sweat welled up on his body, soaking his clothes. Sweat dripped into his eyes and down his nose. His throat was parched. Weights were bearing him down. He wanted to go back, back. They were somewhere here now. They must be. Then an odd sense of calm rose in him. Maybe they've pulled out—altogether, all the way back. Maybe there was nobody.

He was half-way down the field when he heard the click. He hurled himself to the ground as a machine-gun crashed. Then another. There were screams behind him. Then running. Numbly he hugged the earth. Lena! Lena! The stabbing chattering of the guns suddenly ceased. It was silent, as if nothing had happened. Insects buzzed around his head and steeped themselves in the sweat on his neck. Get out, get back. He knew the artillery and mortars would begin blasting as soon as they got the range. Cautiously, he swiveled around on his belly and began to crawl hand over hand, listening through the buzz of the insects. Nothing. He crawled. Our artillery. Then theirs. Get out, out.

He began to see a patch of olive drab. Then a figure, sprawled face dawn, arms outflung, came into sight. It was Gaston, dead. He maneuvered around him, face averted, his eyes level with the fine white stems of the thick grass.

A faint moaning startled him until he realized that it had come from someone ahead. As he crawled, the moaning became more distinct. Again olive drab. He could tell by the combat boots that it was the Lieutenant. Only the Lieutenant had them.

Merrington was lying on his back, his head propped up by his helmet.

"Maniscelloni!" he whispered. "Oh."

He dropped his head back and arched his neck in pain. His trousers were torn and burned on both thighs and soaked with blood.

Sal crawled closer.

"They didn't get me, do you hear?"

Tears welled in the Lieutenant's eyes, then faded. Sweat had turned his shirt almost black. His head swayed.

Sal was up to him, even with his wounded thighs.

"Boy scout," he muttered. His chest muscles ached as he ripped off the Lieutenant's trouser and underwear legs, baring the wounds. He pulled out his first aid dressings and the Lieutenant's and bound them over the shattered thighs.

Merrington moaned. Murmuring, he reached out to grip Sal's shoulder with his hand. Sal shook his fingers off as if they were dry leaves.

He worked his way up to face the Lieutenant. He lay still for a moment recovering his breath. The Lieutenant's eyes were open—heavy and glazed.

Sal looked at him with steady gaze. The Lieutenant's head began to jerk. His face crumpled and the tears came pouring.

"Nuts! The faster you kick off, the better I'll like it, you bastard."

He rolled himself over with his back to the Lieutenant and then pulled himself around with the Lieutenant on his back. The Lieutenant screamed.

"Aw, shut up," Sal said.

He crawled a few inches, then panting, face down, rested. Then he began again. Every pebble, every blade of grass seemed an obstacle. Why? Why am I doing it? He crawled as if he were burrowing through sheer earth. The Lieutenant, who had fainted, was a dead weight pressing him into the ground.

Harry, 1943

Nightshirt in the Ardennes

It had been a fierce, exhausting day for Captain Vanador. Like the other days since the German breakthrough in the Ardennes, its overpowering demands had numbed his body and mind with fatigue.

But now at dusk the claws of tension loosened. The prayed-for planes had finally been able to come out that morning—the wild mad planes, eating Nazi men and metal until the whole moving flame of their offensive, wanting fuel, was reduced from a blaze to a flicker. At last the American ground forces could stop retreating and stabilize their front.

Captain Vanador sat wearily on the snow-covered ground behind a boulder designated as his command post. Although the weather was freezing, sweat trickled down his dark, tense face. His olive drab Mackinaw with the collar turned up on his neck to the edge of his helmet was stiff with frozen mud. He leaned back with his gloved hands in the snow up to the wrists. The Krauts were being held at last. He looked up into the darkening evening sky and caught the flickers of the early stars. Good weather again tomorrow. Flying weather. Good. Good.

The roar of guns was dying down. His ears could listen to the explosions now without pain. The sharp twangings, the hissings inside his head, and the brain-racking concussions were gone now, leaving only echoes. He breathed deeply, rubbing his hot, dry lips with snow.

Little Beagle, the "300" radio set man, came alive on the phone.

"It's the Colonel for you, Captain," he mumbled. His hand shook with cold as he passed the instrument to Vanador.

"Fine work, Van," the colonel was saying. "Fine work. That was some going. I got one commander I can rely on."

Vanador grunted. Involuntarily he bowed his head to the ground as an enemy shell suddenly hit some nearby trees and burst. Jagged steel sang hideously amid crackling, falling branches. Vanador pressed the cold earphone closer.

"Yeah," he said, "but my personnel is all knocked to hell. Only one officer left outside of myself. I need men and bad."

"Pretty tight," said the colonel. "But I got some replacements coming up tonight."

"Jesus, that's great. Where'd you get 'em, out of a cemetery?"

"Colored volunteers from the rear echelons," said the colonel.

"Jesus, no," said Vanador.

"Tough to take when you're from Carolina, I know, Van. But that's what's been sent up and that's what you'll take. This line has got to be held now."

"Yes, sir," said Vanador.

"O.K." The colonel signed off.

Vanador sat up and handed the phone back to Beagle.

"My aching back. Black troops. Twelve years in the National Guard. Four years in the United States Army and now I got black troops. Hell of a war this is getting to be."

"Yes air," said Beagle. "Wish it was over. Wish I was home all right."

"Beagle," Vanador said, "go on over to Lieutenant Wass and tell him to get the connecting file out. And hurry up back. Wanna go to sleep. I'm tired of the whole damn thing. Black troops. My God."

At dawn Vanador was awakened by Lieutenant James just arriving with his platoon of replacements.

"Sorry to wake you up, Captain," Lieutenant James said, "but I thought you'd want to assign us right away."

"Yeah," Vanador said, rubbing his mouth. Just like this kind to wake me up. Couldn't just sit around and wait a while, oh no.

He glanced at the lieutenant standing above him. Big fellow. Light brown mug. The arrogant, near-white kind. All decked out in combat dress, trying to look like a soldier.

"Git down here, Lieutenant," Vanador said. "You're at the front now, not in some laundry outfit in the rear. You keep on standing up that way and the next thing we know those Krauts'll be shooting away at us like mad."

"Yes sir" the Lieutenant said and hurriedly kneeled down next to the captain.

"Look," said Vanador, pulling soggy maps out of his Mackinaw pocket and spreading them open. "Come down close under this boulder where I can put my flash on these. Here. This here is our position. This is your part of the front, got it? The left flank of the company front."

"Yes, sir."

"You gotta watch out for tank attacks. The Krauts are great for feelin' us out at a time like this. Fight them tanks off. Keep those men of yours in their positions. They gotta be held at all costs, understand?"

"Yes, sir."

"Any questions?"

Lieutenant James seemed to think a minute.

"No, sir."

"Know everything. huh?" Vanador said.

"No, sir." Lieutenant James said, "I certainly don't. I'll ask questions as they come up."

"Well, get going now. Down that path to the brook and you'll be where you ought to be."

Vanador turned his back as James rose and in a crouching gait led his men off.

All that day American bombers and fighters smashed away at the enemy. As long as the planes were out Vanador knew that the Nazis would not dare attack. But at dusk when the droning had ceased, just as he expected, the German artillery opened up on his company. With hissing gibberish shell after shell crashed in.

Vanador cautiously peered over the edge of the boulder through his field glasses. In the dimming light he could make out three tiger tanks racing towards James' positions. Their machine guns were going full blast.

How the hell do they know where to go, Vanador thought as he grabbed the company radio.

"James," he said into the mouthpiece. "James, listen."

"Yes, sir." James controlled, educated voice grated in his ear."

"James. Get your bazookas and antitank grenades ready. Don't fire until those tanks are close up."

"Yes, sir."

Vanador threw himself flat on the ground as a shell howled nearby and burst with a deafening crack.

"Keep those men of yours in their position, do you hear. No runnin' away, understand?" Vanador shouted into the phone, getting back to the edge of the boulder.

"Yes, sir."

Vanador held the phone tight against his ear while straining his eyes to watch the dark moving forms of the tanks. They were coming closer and closer.

"Now open up, open up!" he roared into the phone.

There was no answer.

"James, God damn it, open up."

The tanks were almost on top of James' position, pouring out machine gun fire.

"You sonofabitch," Vanador said.

Suddenly James' position rocked with bazooka blasts, machine gun and rifle fire and the crash of anti-tank grenades. One of the tanks, exploding, stopped dead. Another spun around abruptly and fled back, firing as it went. The third plunged straight into James' position. Then it too stopped dead. There was wild firing, an explosion, and then silence.

"James" Vanador said into the phone, "damn you, are you listening?"

"Yes, sir," James voice came through.

"What the hell were you doing? Why wasn't you on the radio?"

"I wanted to make sure of getting a couple of those tanks."

"That ain't what I told you to do."

"Well, the opportunity came up so I—"

"Opportunity hell," Vanador interrupted. "Listen you, you better learn to take orders."

"I did. I just used my judgment when I saw there wasn't any infantry behind those tanks. I figured the Nazis were just trying to feel us out, like you said."

"All you was supposed to do was drive those tanks off."

"Even if I could get a couple?"

"You think you were smart, Well let me tell you, you were just goddam insubordinate."

"Yes, sir."

Vanador violently threw down the phone.

After dark the colonel called on the "300" set.

"Van? I saw that business with the tanks. Good going. Somebody over there deserves a decoration. Get a patrol out tonight and look around. Find out what they've got there."

Yeah, Vanador thought, after the colonel had signed off, yeah. Deserves a decoration. I'd decorate him all right. He jerked his carbine off his shoulder and, standing up, fired into the night ahead. Then he pulled the empty clip out, clamped in a full one with a bang and fired again in a burst. I'd decorate him, just like that, he said to himself.

A flare from the German lines flowered in the sky opposite the company front, hanging like a ghostly chandelier.

Vanador slumped down behind his boulder.

"Beagle," he said to his radio man, "get that Lieutenant James here just as soon as that flare dies out."

He leaned his head against the boulder and stared into the sky. He'd show that James just what he was.

James was beside him suddenly.

"Yes, sir?" he said.

"It's you," Vanador said. "You're goin' out with me on a reconnaissance patrol. Set your watch with mine. We'll leave at one-forty."

"One-forty," James said.

"We're gonna look around. Maybe you'll learn something you don't know. There are a few things I can show you, boy."

James didn't reply.

Vanador stretched his long legs.

"We'll find out what they've got and come back—if we can."

James was silent for a moment, then he cleared his throat and said,

"I know what they've got out there—a lot of tanks, some machine gun positions and infantry."

Vanador stiffened.

"How the hell do you know?"

James stuck the thumb of his right hand under his carbine sling.

"I went out after dark and took a look around."

"You did, huh. Who asked you to go?"

"No one, sir, but I thought—"

"You thought. You're not supposed to think. Your job is to lead your platoon. I'll do all the thinkin' for you. In my home town people like you are not allowed to think."

"We're not in your home town, Captain," James said quietly.

Vanador pushed his helmet back furiously.

'"No?"

"No," said James.

Vanador sat back very still, thinking. Then he said, "We're goin' on a patrol tonight—a combat patrol, Lieutenant, a fighting combat patrol."

"Yes," Lieutenant James said.

"I'm taking the whole company except Wass and his platoon. He'll give us cover if we need it. You're gonna go down your side along the brook. I'll go down my side here along the mound."

"Then what?" James said.

Vanador looked at him sharply, "Then we'll sneak right into their lines and tear up everything we can."

James tugged hard at his carbine sling with his thumb.

"With everything they got out there? I don't see how."

"You don't, don't you? Well, the hell with you then," Vanador said.

"If we go out there and get wiped out then tomorrow all those

Krauts will have to do is just walk through here right up to regiment. This place'll be wide open. You can't do that, Captain."

"You take your orders and mind your own business."

"I do. But your plan has no sense unless—" James raised his voice.

"Unless what?"

"Unless your only aim is to see how many of us you can get killed no matter what happens after."

"You're yellow, Lieutenant, you're afraid to go." Vanador said.

"Not yellow, but black—that's the point."

"Goddamit," Vanador said, "shut your ass and get this straight. I'm the Commanding Officer here. Go back to your platoon and brief your men. And if there is any holding back for any reason I'll hold you responsible and charge you with desertion in line of duty, understand?"

James let go of his carbine sling.

"I understand," he said in a firm voice, "I sure do."

"Now get out," Vanador said, spitting. "I'll see that Wass gets his orders and we'll start at one-forty."

At exactly one-forty Vanador led his men out of their positions into the dark. By peering very hard he could faintly make out James' platoon starting along the brook. Into the dark, Vanador kept moving slowly, listening, watching.

"Keep 'em moving," he said to his sergeant, "keep 'em moving. Let the men hold onto each others' belts."

In single file the men followed behind him, step by step.

An enemy flare opened in the sky in eerie silence. Vanador and his men stood stock still in the weird pallid light. That long line over there, Vanador thought, that must be James and his monkeys. They'll show what they are as soon as the Krauts open up. They'll just run and get it right, good and damn right. The flare died out. Vanador started his men going again.

"They musta spotted us, Cap," the sergeant whispered nervously, "it's too darn quiet."

"Shut up," said Vanador, "just shut up."

A German machine gun ripped into the silence. Vanador and his men hit the ground and began to crawl. Over to the left another machine gun opened up. That's for James, Vanador thought. He listened beneath the metallic drilling for sounds of confusion. There were none. Bastards are still holding out. It's that lousy James. But he'll crack soon. He's got to.

The guns stopped. Vanador crawled faster. First one leg then the other. The men behind him followed.

A plane's buzz began to emerge from the German lines, getting relentlessly louder. The sound pressed into his head as the plane, suddenly visible, swooped down close, then turned around and up and down again over James and his platoon. Then finally soaring up and back towards the German lines with a receding buzz.

"They've got us spotted," the sergeant said, "they've got us spotted. That's the whole Kraut army right there."

"Shut up," Vanador said.

They began to move again. James still there, Vanador thought, still there. Why the hell don't they get up and run back like they should and get killed—the yellow bastards.

Now there was only the sound of bodies dragging over the snow. Vanador bumped his helmet against barbed wire. Close now. Almost there. James. James at the wire too. Come on, James, I dare you. He lifted the wire cautiously and crawled under.

Suddenly machine guns burst—in front, on the left, on the right, across the field. Vanador hugged the snow-covered earth fiercely as the slugs snipped overhead. He could hear screams of pain from across the field. Now they're caught, good and caught. Behind him men were screaming too. The front became alive with whispering, snarling sounds followed by explosions and horrible human cries.

He can't move any more. Not any more, he can't. I've got him, I've got him. Vanador leaped to his feet and shouted into the racket across the field.

"Come on, James. you bastard, come on."

No answer came. Exultantly, furiously, he rushed forward firing his carbine. His feet caught in the wire. No heard German voices close by as he struggled wildly to free himself. A machine gun blasted at him suddenly, riddling him with slugs.

Freedom

Although he knew that Marion was anxiously awaiting his arrival, Joel made no haste in getting dressed that noon. In fact one might accuse him of stalling in completing that process. He dawdled over putting on his socks and shoes, after having shaved at a pace that was something less than leisurely. He coughed and fretted as he adjusted his collar and tie with awkward, slipping fingers. Especially when he thought of Marion waiting for him he became numb with a strange dual sensation which, while impelling him to hurry to her, at the same time restrained him from doing that very thing. It was born of the awkward situation in which he found himself. Marion, at the end of a long, breathless kiss, had promised her impatient lover, with a touch of melodrama, "everything" for this very afternoon. Joel recalled almost too vividly for the state of his inflamed desire how she had done so, just before he had left Tuesday night. It had been a most exquisite, ego-satisfying moment. But why did she have to spoil it all, Joel thought of himself, by insisting, quite prosaically, that he must come to dinner at three? Why couldn't she understand, drat her, that Saturday dinner was a sacred rite to his mother, although he usually got up so late that he had to eat it alone. But she had insisted and he had acceded, thinking weakly that he would deal with the matter when it came up. And now that it had to be dealt with at once he was somewhat baffled. It was the psychological brake that was slowing down his entire dressing process. It got tangled up with everything he did.

He couldn't rid himself of the problem. He tried to stow it away in some obscure corner of his mind where it would be quiescent, using, to suppress it, such weights as, "If I don't wanna eat dinner at home to-day what affair of mom's is it anyway? Besides, I'm twenty-one and I ought to have some rights around here."

But it kept bobbing up like a cork in a basin of water. He knew that inevitably he would have to face the crisis, in fact just as soon as he finished his irresolute dressing.

The aroma of frying chicken, ordinarily a fragrance that put him in a happy mood (he was fond of his meals), vexed him to-day as it floated into his room. Somehow it got tangled up in his mind with Marion. He swore at her silently, mildly, —restrained by some intuitive sense of delicacy from using harsh words of profanity—for getting him into this pickle. His mother, he realized, already suspected that he was in the midst of an affair. His late hours and his neglected college work, coupled with his friend Sam's indiscrete remarks in her presence about Marion, had already provided her with plenty of evidence. All she needed to clinch the case in her mind, probably, was this going out for dinner this afternoon.

In the midst of his thoughts he heard his mother's footsteps, soft and ominous on the carpeted floor, approach his room. He braced himself for the knock which came a moment later. And then a peculiarly calm voice, which in its very restraint was an exasperating challenge of battle to him, said,

"Joel dear, dinner is ready, so hurry up. I don't want to stand in a hot kitchen all day."

Joel strode uneasily to the door, opened it with an awkward twist of his hand and confronted his mother as if she were a foe. But at the last moment he faltered in his resolution to have it out then and there.

"I just had breakfast, mom. I can't eat again so soon. I'm not at all hungry," he said lamely with a trace of a whine in his voice.

His mother looked at him impassively as if she had been expecting just such an answer and had already made provision to meet the emergency.

"Well, I'll keep it warm. Fried chicken will stand. Just tell me when you want it and I'll have it ready," she replied, smiling as she turned away. He caught the curious look in her eyes that contradicted the smile. And a sudden gust of depression swept through him.

It nursed the growing tension in his mind, the desire with which his emotions had been flaming seemed to have been suddenly extinguished. Again he felt a strong resentment against Marion for the dilemma she had created for him. Strangely, it was accompanied by a feeling of shame. For a moment the idea that Marion was no better than a whore disturbed him. And his mother—why must she thwart him and try so subtly to reassert her power over him? What a damn coward he was. Why couldn't he say to his mother, "See here, mom, I'm a man and I'm gonna lead my own life. So please don't interfere in my affairs." It pleased him, for the moment, to imagine himself telling this to his mother and subduing her with one blow. But actually he knew that he couldn't. he would have to resort to less direct means.

He donned his hat and coat in exasperation, bracing himself for another set-to with his mother.

"What time are you coming home, Joel?" his mother asked quietly, almost cajolingly, ignoring the fundamental question of dinner for the moment, as he stopped at the kitchen door before leaving.

"Aw, I don't know. Pretty late I guess." The whine was more pronounced this time. He knew that his mother would get around to the dinner presently. And so she did.

"So you're not eating at home?"

"No."

"Well then what are you going to do for dinner? You'll certainly be hungry not eating all day," she asked almost gaily.

She just had to know. For a moment he felt impelled to lie. But he restrained himself out of deference to his own claims to having reached manhood. To lie would be to reduce himself to childhood again, to justify his mother in reasserting her power over him. He inwardly stiffened, his entire being set on asserting his will, on his right to do as he pleased.

"I've been invited out to dinner," he answered almost fiercely, pulling on the brim of his hat. He noticed the woebegone look on his mother's face. Now she knew. He felt a sudden swell of emotion through his body.

He expected her to berate him for not telling her sooner, and to put him through the usual inquisition. But she merely asked, almost timidly, as if afraid of the answer,

"With one of the boys?"

"NO," he said, stressing the word by letting it pop out of his mouth. Now she knew and knew.

His mother was silent. Her face betrayed her unhappiness. Joel unexpectedly felt, in this moment of victory, an immense sorrow for her. Only by an effort, and by another mental reference to his adult pretensions did he manage to restrain himself from capitulating and staying home. After all, he wished to defeat her gently, not to crush her. He wished to free himself, without thereby enslaving her, not realizing that to lose power is to be subjugated.

Joel bit his lip and pulled furiously at the brim of his hat as he prepared to leave.

"Be back about ten o'clock," he said, as he left, throwing her a bone of consolation in the form of this one definite piece of information, adding, immediately regretful of this unmanly weakness, "—if any of the boys should call and ask."

At last he was free. Now he could go to Marion.

On his way to the subway station, by way of aphrodisiac he tried to revive his romantic mood. But most vexingly, the image of Marion that his mind conjured up filled him with a kind of repulsion. And he stopped, staring absently down the street, trying to find out why. Did he love Marion, or was here merely infatuated—sex-possessed? He stood loitering by the street corner, beneath a billboard blaring to the passersby this week's attractions at the neighborhood movie theater. Hadn't she told him at one critical moment, after a passionate, scent-filled, mouthy kiss, that she had lived with another man for several years? It had been enough at the moment to make him tender and love even more this brave, brave girl who defied convention to love as she chose. It fitted perfectly his adolescent-adult ideal of complete freedom. Now she seemed to be something different.

"I'll call a spade a spade," he said to himself fiercely. "Why, she's no better than a whore."

With pride he thought that he knew something about life now. It ought not to be gawped at through the prism of romance.

He didn't want to go to Marion now. What had eating dinner to do with sexual desire? He saw it all now, he thought to himself, as he looked back. It was all a snare. To eat dinner at Marion's would be to subjugate himself to her. That's what he was trying to run away from. He had just fought a mighty battle with his mother. And for what? To run straight into a situation precisely like the one he had just escaped? Not he.

Suddenly he started walking again, away from the station. He felt immensely relieved as he paid twenty-five cents to see the latest attraction at the neighborhood theater.

And he thought to himself as he sat down in the darkened theater, "Well, I'll surprise mom and have dinner at home—."

Harry, 1929

POEM

We sat so long at banquet tables
So many years we spent with words
And paintings, and fixed on pubic hair,
Brushed our legs with silk and gold.
So long softened our buttocks on green
padded mahogany chairs,
Enjoyed hot showers, faux leather, blondes,
plush Pullman cars,
Clawed for fame and adored the rising bank account.
Journeyed and ruminated all the while
And gathered hate and prejudice to etch out
Lugoric images in our minds.
And turned to skulls and bones,
Juxtaposed the dear and drear,
Poured blood on life,
Learned the art of vendetta,
Of betrayal of friends,
Found the exaltations with the rejection
Of the sacrament to bless-curse it all.
And Death was the revered.

But now we have met the eighty-eight
And are wise with the knowledge of ?nebelivefers?
And schmissers and burp guns and Messerschmidts
And potato-mashers, knee mortars, Zeroes
And M.G.-42s

And oh—the man behind us, his color doesn't
Matter. And his race is man.
And oh, please dear dea—Reds of Russia get to
Berlin first.

Oh the wonders of life! Coca-Cola, hamburgers,
Hot dogs, steaks and french fries, ice cream, beer,
Movie palaces, a sweet girl (I'll marry her and have
Five kids), a job, an auto, any part of the United States.

I'll obey the Ten Commandments,
I'll follow Christ's Sermon on the Mount.
Who cares for fame? The impression-making phrase?
My I.Q. doesn't matter.
I want to live.

Oh you dried-up ones, you liars—
You sighers, you skull and bones, you
Swastika wavers, you false sacrament
Sayers. You ???? killers and lynchers. You
America-Firsters and me-firsters.
Go to the graves you have dug for us.
Death is for you, not for us.

V-mails and Letters, 1944

The following are letters from Harry Rutkoff to his family, all addressed to "Mr. and Mrs. S. Rutkoff—865 Walton Ave.—Bronx, N.Y." They were sent by V-Mail from England and from mainland Europe, during the months of May through September, 1944.

"During the latter years of World War II, V-Mail became a popular way to correspond with a loved one serving overseas. V-Mail letters were written on forms that could be purchased at five and ten cent stores or the post office. (Once filled-in with a handwritten or typed letter, and carefully addressed and folded) these forms were photographed, put on film, flown across the world and then reproduced at the mail center closest to the recipient's position. (When reprinted from film, each V-Mail letter measured roughly 4 by 5 inches in size.)

"The development of the V-Mail system reduced the time it took a soldier to receive a letter by a month—from six weeks by boat to twelve days or less by air. However, the main advantage of V-Mail was its compact nature. Reduction in the size and weight of the letters translated into more space for crucial military supplies on cargo planes; one advertisement explained that 1,700 V-Mail letters could fit in a cigarette packet, while reducing the weight of the letters in paper form by 98%. Transport of the letters by plane minimized the chances that the enemy would intercept the letters, although writers were reminded to delete any information that might prove useful to the enemy in case some V-Mail was captured.

"Americans on the home-front were encouraged by the government and private businesses to use V-Mail. Letters from home were compared to 'a five minute furlough,' and advertisements that instructed how, when, and what to write in a V-Mail reached a peak in 1944. Letters were to be cheerful, short, and frequent. V-Mail made it possible for servicemen halfway across the world to hear news from home on a weekly basis." (John W. Hartman Center for Sales, Advertising, and Marketing History, Duke University Rare Book, Manuscript, and Special Collections Library.)

V-Mails and Letters

FROM: Pvt. H. Rutkoff, 42052120
Co. D, Int. APO 15-305
c/o Postmaster, N.Y.

V-⋯-MAIL

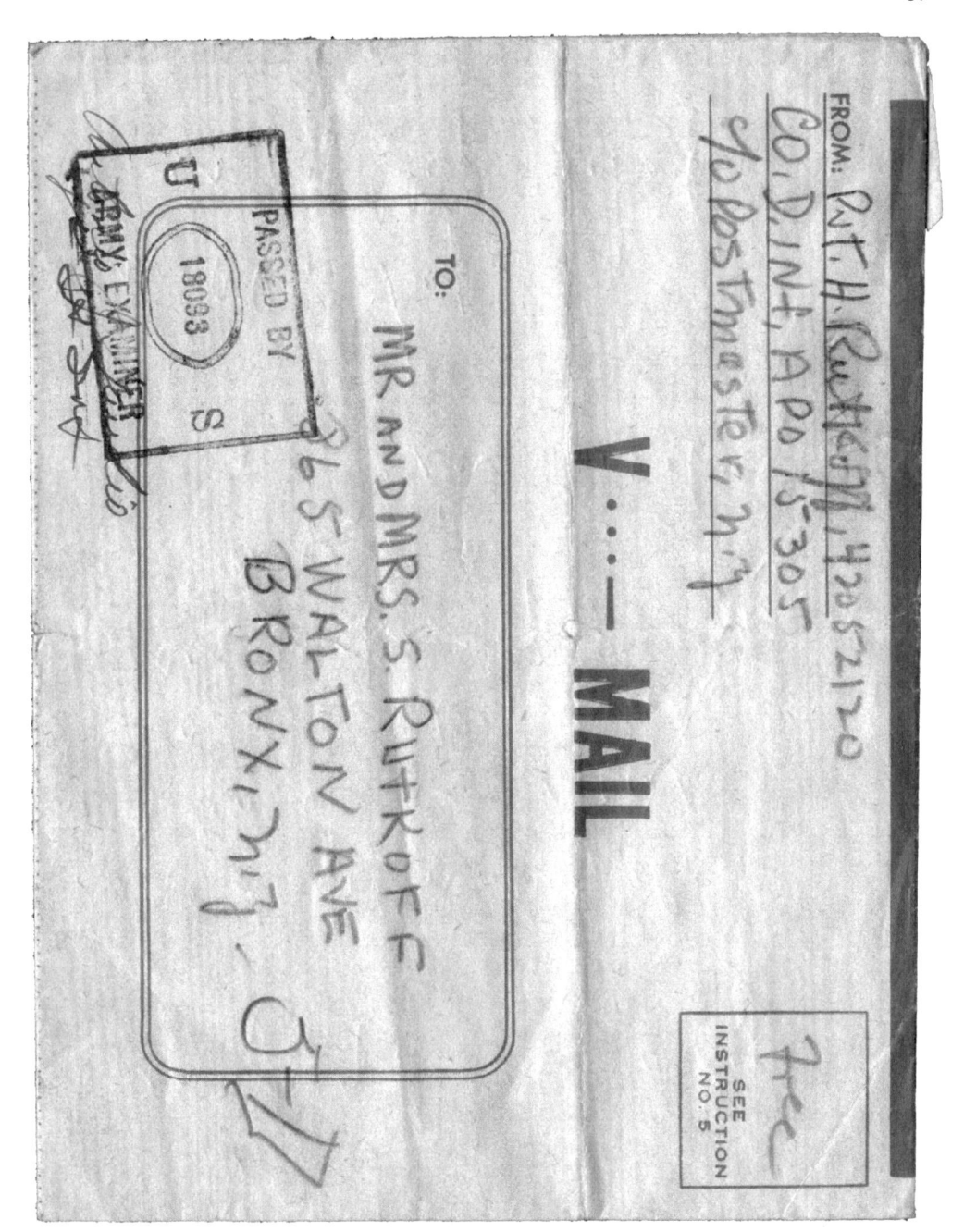

TO:
MR and MRS. S. RUTKOFF
965 WALTON AVE
BRONX, N.Y.

PASSED BY
18083
U   S

ARMY EXAMINER

Free

SEE INSTRUCTION NO. 5

38 HARRY RUTKOFF

FROM: Pvt. H. Rutkoff, 42052120
CO. D. Inf, APO 15305
℅ Postmaster, N.Y.

Free
SEE INSTRUCTION NO. 5

V — MAIL

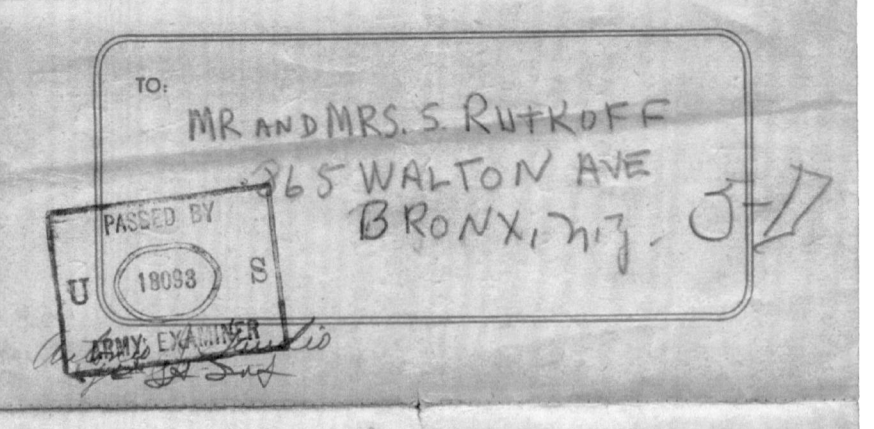

TO:
MR AND MRS. S. RUTKOFF
865 WALTON AVE
BRONX, N.Y.

PASSED BY
U 18093 S
ARMY EXAMINER

V-Mail service provides a most rapid means of communication. If addressed to a place where photographing service is not available the original letter will be dispatched by the most expeditious means.

INSTRUCTIONS

(1) Write the entire message plainly on the other side within marginal lines.

(2) Print the name and address in the two spaces provided. Addresses of members of the Armed Forces should show full name, complete military or naval address, including grade or rank, serial number, unit to which assigned or attached and army post office in care of the appropriate postmaster or appropriate fleet post office.

(3) Fold, seal, and deposit in any post office letter drop or street letter box.

(4) Enclosures must not be placed in this envelope.

(5) V-Mail letters may be sent free of postage by members of the Armed Forces. When sent by others postage must be prepaid at domestic rates (3c ordinary mail, 6c if domestic air mail service is desired when mailed in the U. S.)

☆ GPO 16—28143-4

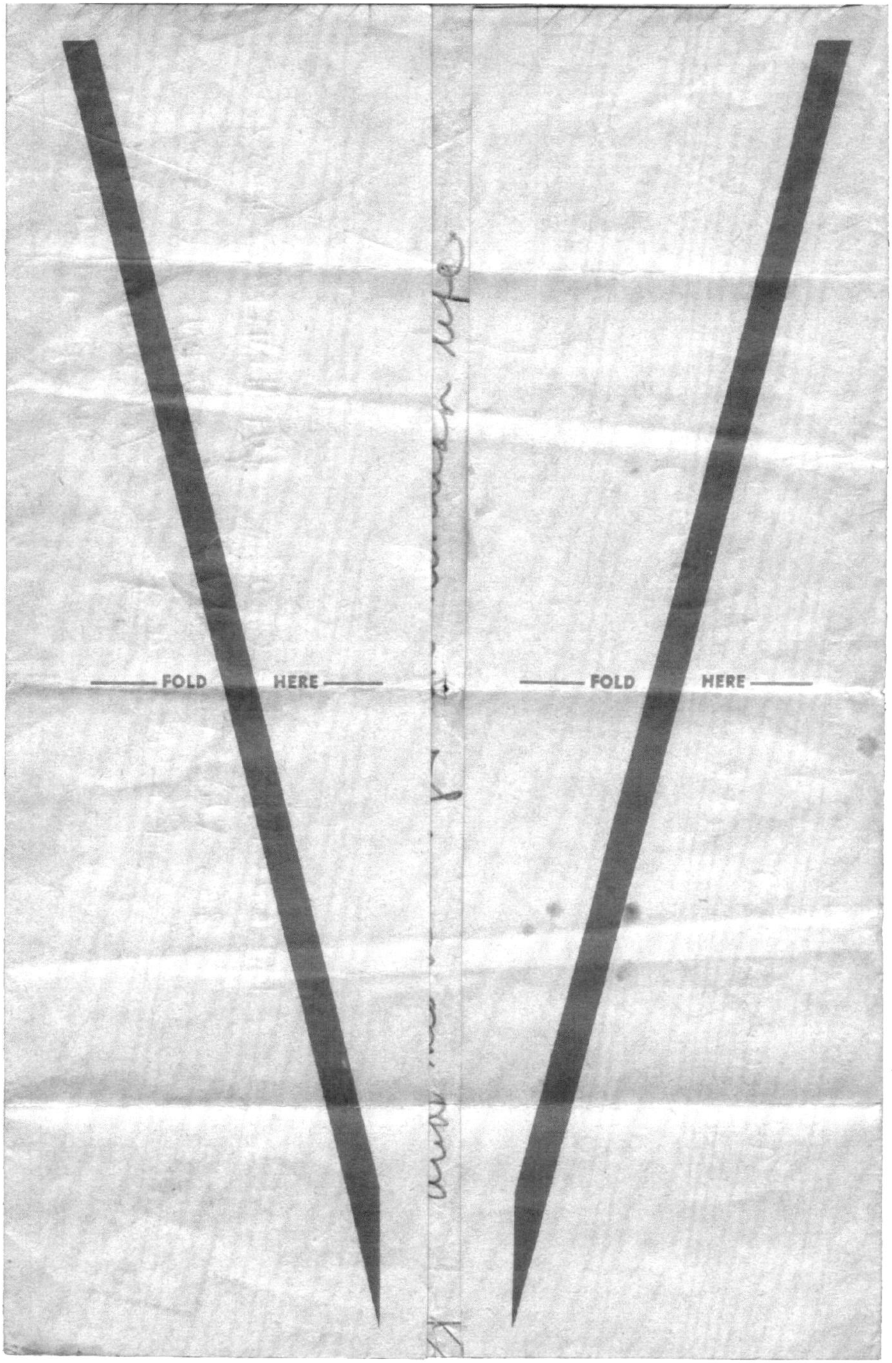
FOLD HERE
FOLD HERE

V-Mail—May 28, 1944
Dear Mom, Pop and Ann,
The part of England I'm in is very beautiful. It's the kind off countryside that people dream about—beautiful meadows with thick green grass, wild flowers like buttercups, daisys. The trees are old and beautiful. Some are very tall and reach right up into the blue skies. You'd never think there was a war on.

My life here is healthy and I feel fine.

I hope you are all well and are not worrying too much. Except for slowness in getting mail it's as if I were someplace in the U.S. So don't worry.

Love,
Harry
P.S. Please send me some candy.

Harry, Peter, Minnie—1943

V-Mail—May 30, 1944
Dear Mom, Pop, Ann,
I hope you are all well and are taking care of yourselves and that you are taking care of my Minnie and my Peter for me. I'm fine and dandy and in the peak of condition.

Peter's birthday is next Monday. I'll bet he'll have a cake with two candles. Well, I pine for him all right, but so do many, many other daddies pine for their kids in this army.

It's raining cats and dogs this evening in typical English style.
All my love,
Harry

V-Mail—June 1, 1944
Dear Mom, Pop, Ann,

In England the traffic signs say "Halt" instead of "Stop." A place where you stop for beer is a "pub" instead of a saloon. And it's surprising how many English people are red-heads.

We get all the news from home here in an Army newspaper called the "Stars and Stripes" and it's a very good newspaper. It comes out every day. English newspapers are not as good.

Altho I haven't received your last box of candy as yet, here is a request for another box.

All my love,
Harry

V-Mail—undated
Dear Mom, Pop, Ann,

The other day I visited an English town and got a pair picture of what it is like to live here. People are surprisingly small. In fact everything is small in size. But there are lots and lots of trees and every house no matter how poor, has its little garden with plenty of flowers which people tend carefully. Most of the people around are either very young or old. The others are "busy" as you can read in the papers.

Peter and Minnie by now are at the beach. I hope it won't be too hard for Mom and Pop to visit them.

Take care of yourselves and don't worry.
I'm fine.
All my love,
Harry

V-Mail—June 11, 1944
Dear Mom, Pop, Ann,
The weather here is abominable. It rains and rains and finally gets into your bones.

What happened to Ann? Is she all right? Please write me all about it.

Minnie writes me full reports on Peter's progress. I'm sure proud of him. What wouldn't I give to see him.

I also enjoy Mom's letters about our Peter.

I'm fine and have nothing to kick about. Don't worry about me. I'll be all right.

I guess you know the invasion is on. It means the beginning of the end for Hitler. May the end come soon.

All my love,
Harry

V-Mail—June 18, 1944
Dear Mom, Pop, Ann,
I see by the newspapers that the first phase of the Great Invasion is a great success. Let's hope it keeps up and that the end of the Nazis comes soon.

I feel fine and am pretty comfortable. I live in a tent. But since it is summer it is rather nice. It gets quite cold here at night and it's pretty damp. Otherwise the country-side is beautiful.

I hope that Ann is all better and has recovered from her fall.

Don't worry, Mom, everything will be all right.

All my love,
Your Harry

Pop, write once in a while.

V-Mail—June 21, 1944
Dear Mom, Pop, Ann,
I hope that by now Ann's back is all better.
I am fine. I'm eating well, and sleeping well and enjoying life as far as that's possible in the Army.
Altho to-day is the first day of summer here you'd hardly know it, especially in the morning it's cold enough to wear your overcoat.
Over here, as you are at home, I am greatly interested in the Invasion. I'll bet it made some splash in good ole New York when the news came thru.
Don't worry. I'll be all right.
Love,
Harry

V-Mail—June 23, 1944
Dear Mom, Pop, Ann,
The weather in England is improving at last. To-day really seems almost like summer. There's a joke about England's weather, that it has three seasons,—early winter, winter, and late winter. That's almost true.
My health is excellent. I don't know that I've grown any muscles lately working but I'm kept busy.
I hope Ann's back is better. And that Mom feels O.K. and is not worrying too much.
Take care, as I know you are, of Peter and Minnie for me.
All my love,
Harry

44 HARRY RUTKOFF

TO: Mr and Mrs S. Rutkoff
865 Walton Ave.
Bronx, N.Y.

FROM: Pvt. H. Rutkoff, 42052120
Co. D. Inf, APO 15305
c/o Postmaster, N.Y.
July 12, 1944

Dear Mom Pop Ann,

Well, well, — here it is July 12 already. See how time flies.

I have been separated from my old tent mate and now I have a new one. His name is Leonard Weintraub and he's a lawyer in civilian life. Curiously enough he comes from Minnie's old neighborhood in Brooklyn.

I'm fine and feel well. Life is not very hard and is pretty quiet here.

Don't worry and take care of yourselves.

All My Love,
Harry

V-Mail—July 17, 1944
Dear Mom, Pop, Ann,
This is the first chance I've had to write in several days. Don't worry if I don't write for a while every so often. It's not that I don't want to. It's only that I'm stuck for time.
Note the change in my address.
I feel fine and well. Don't worry. Everything will be all right.
All my love,
Harry

V-Mail—undated
Dear Mom, Pop, Ann,
Hello kids.
The weather is changeable as ever. You'd think things would improve in France. But no, the weather is the same here as in England.
French kids like all kids are always looking for candy.
I'm so very glad you are having a good time with Peter.
Please don't worry about me. It doesn't do anyone any good. I'll be as all right as the next fellow. There's a lot of us.
All my love,
Harry

46 THE NEXT HEDGEROW

V-Mail—August 18, 1944
Dear Mom, Pop, Ann,

I suppose Min has told you by now that I have been wounded and that I am in a hospital in England. Don't worry about me because I'm getting magnificent care. My wounds are not crippling or permanently disabling so that's something that should relieve your minds. Furthermore after a while I expect to be shipped to a hospital in the U.S. near home. So that's something to look forward to.

Well, dear parents, life takes these turns in times like these when our enemies are so fierce. I guess we all ought to be glad that my wounds are not worse.

All my love,
Harry

V-Mail—August 24, 1944
Dear Mom, Pop, Ann,

Just a few words to let you know that I am progressing fine. I've undergone a few operations and my wounds are now under control and healing. I have very little pain. All I do is lie in bed and wait for the day when the order will come sending me to a hospital in the U.S. near home to convalesce. Then I'll see all my dear ones.

Don't worry and take care of yourselves. Among other things Hitler's end doesn't seem so far off. Nor Japan's.

All my love,
Harry

V-Mail—August 25, 1944
Dear Mom, Pop, Ann,

A few words to let you know that I'm getting along all right. I've had a few operations and now I'm all patched up. The doctor says that after a while except for a few minor things, I'll be as good as new.

So don't worry about me. I'm very lucky not to be left with anything much permanently wrong.

Take care of yourselves. I hope to see you soon.

The operations were nothing as far as I'm concerned. I just slept thru them. I feel pretty good now. Even eat a lot and sleep at night.

All my love,
Harry

V-Mail—August 28, 1944
Dear Mom, Pop, Ann,

To-day I'm feeling much better. The doctor who is treating me says I'm getting along fine. Pretty soon I ought to be in good enough shape for that boat ride home.

Major Brown, the doctor in charge of my case, is a wonderful guy. In appearance he reminds me of Pop. Even has some of his mannerisms. In skill he's tops and unassuming at that. I'm lucky to have him. As a matter of fact all the doctors at this hospital are swell guys.

Don't worry Mom, your boy will be all right. Take care of Peter and Minnie for me, as you are.

Oh, for a letter from you reassuring me that you're all O.K.

All my love,
Harry

V-Mail—August 31, 1944
Dear Mom, Pop, Ann,

Here is a little bulletin on your son's health—flash—doctor says he is getting along fine. So don't worry. By the way, have an enormous appetite. I don't know if it's because I'm really hungry or whether it's a way out of the boredom of lying in bed.

The war, as you must be reading, is going very well. I think that one of these days pretty soon Germany is going to collapse and the war will be over. That will be a great day for rejoicing, huh?

Chuck Peter under the chin and kiss him for me. Maybe I'll be seeing you all soon.
All my love,
Harry

Letter fragment—September 2, 1944
Dear Mom, Pop, Ann,
This morning I received your letters and, believe me, they made me very happy. It was so good to hear from you and to know that you were taking the news about my being wounded calmly, which is as it should be. I think I will have only a little permanently wrong with me when I'm finally better. I'm not disfigured. All my senses, eyes ears etc. are fine. My legs and arms are all in their proper places. I might have to use a cane for a while because of my broken leg. And be careful of where I sit until my backside heals up. But that's all.
The Colonel looked me over to-day and said I was ready to go home. So as soon as…

V-Mail—September 8, 1944
Dear Mom, Pop, Ann,
Here I am waiting for the old boat home. Yesterday a lot of fellows left for home. So that should push me a little further up the list. Here's hoping there are more loads in the near future heading home.
My doctor says my rear-end is healing very well and probably will not require any further surgery. My leg is—well fractures just take time to heal, that's all. It doesn't bother me except for this darn cast that comes up to my chest. The reason it's so big is that it's supposed to keep my leg in one spot without moving.
Won't I be glad to see you all, especially my Peter.
All my love,
Harry

V-Mail—September 11, 1944

Dear Mom, Pop, Ann,

I'm feeling much better as time goes on. Of course it's no picnic, lying in bed in a big cast but I'm in no particular pain, so don't ever worry on that score.

The weather here is surprisingly changeable—cold at night and warm during the day. Everybody always said England had such a mild climate all year round. Baloney. It's worse than New York.

Of course I just jump with joy every time I think of getting back, but I gotta be patient and wait my turn to go. Each day is a day nearer.

Be good kids and don't worry.

All my love,

Harry

Letter—September 16, 1944

Dear Mom, Pop, Ann,

I'm making good progress in healing up. Don't worry about my pain, it's not much, just discomfort. Nope, Ann, the first week was not painful. I was full of morphine and so didn't feel very much. The worst of this whole thing was being out on the battlefield waiting for the "medicos" to get to me. It took four or five hours. That was my only really tough time. And that was mental, because I had to keep hidden from the Germans whose lines were very close to where I lay. After our artillery knocked them cold and scared my shirt off, the battle was over and I could be rescued. But that happens to almost everybody who gets wounded. Where else can you get wounded but on a battlefield?

…only two hours after I was off the field I already had had two blood transfusions and was in the waiting room of the operating room in the field emergency hospital. The next thing I knew it was the next morning and I was in an airplane over the English Channel.

V-Mail—September 18, 1944
Dear Mom, Pop, Ann,
All your letters are eagerly grabbed when they arrive. If a day passes without mail from Ann, Min or Mom it's a sad day indeed. It's too bad Gramps is not a writing man. If he were he could tell me his adventures with Peter.

My progress here is good. I eat well and get more than enough. I'm just lying around now waiting for the old boat. Soon, soon. So be patient.

I answered Aunt Fanny's letter so that ought to please Mom. I was glad to hear from Aunt Fanny anyhow.

Life here isn't all hospital gloom. Like Americans soldiers everywhere we have our fun no matter what. I have made a number of friends here and we jabber away when we are comfortable enough, or kid one another about our wounds or pains.

All my love,
Harry

V-Mail—September 21, 1944
Dear Mom, Pop, Ann,
I'll try to write you more letters. Only there isn't very much to say. All I'm doing now is waiting for a boat to take me home. That might take weeks so don't get impatient. But I'll be home and that's the important thing, isn't it?

I feel pretty good, altho lying in bed for six and a half weeks, four of them with this cast, is getting to be tiresome. But I've been a good guy about it, haven't I? By the time I get home I'll probably be out of this cast and in a small one.

That time you picked it, Mom, in the newsreel and the Times mag. Story. There I was. I admit it was sort of rough. But we licked the lice, didn't we?

All my love,
Harry

Harry, 1946—Fort Dix

Minnie & Peter, 1943

Peter Rutkoff: Story

Peter, 1968—Paris

Deux Marc

Her gold bracelet sparkles. It's the brightest thing in the dreary room. Like every Party meeting he's ever been to workers cram the place. Their faces pale with exhaustion and their wool caps shadow their eyes. Except for this smart woman, like a film star taking a pint with the help, she shares the table with the proletariat. *Comme c'est vivante,* alive, Marc thinks about her bracelet. A dozen hoops jangle up from her slender wrist, catching on her black blouse as she lifts her hand and waves it from the back. The burly man sitting next to Marc in the front of the hall calls her name, "Francie, yes."

"I think it would be swell to have him. I mean we can," she pauses, her eyes moist, "now that Dan's home on weekend furlough. We'd love to have Monsieur Zitron stay with us." She pronounces Marc's name like the car he owned before the war. Necks crane to look at the woman who has spoken from the last row.

The man next to Marc, his nubby wool suit threadbare and damp, shifts in his chair and glances at Marc as he speaks to the woman in the gold bracelet, "Very kind of you, Francie. Very kind. The Party is grateful for your generosity. Your usual generosity." He looks around the room and finds the nods of approval. Francie smiles, and Marc feels her sad eyes on him. She brings her arm down, hiding the gold hoops between her crossed wrists. She intrigues him, this blonde American communist.

"Daddy's …"
"Shush, it's not him."
"… home!"

The words slide under the door into his sleep. Marc startles at their presence. He swings his feet out of bed and finds the floor. He takes in the room, then glances out over Central Park where the forsythia blooms like butter. The wind from across the park swells the pale curtains that frame the room's two French doors. They open with large brass handles and for a moment he imagines that he is still in Paris, on rue Monsieur le Prince. He rubs the dark stubble on his cheek and walks over to the doors. Leaning out he braces his hands on the black wrought-iron railing, reaches into the pocket of his wrinkled khaki trousers and slips the pale yellow cylinder of a cigarette from its green packet. He stands for a moment, searching, the Galois dangling from his lips.

"Please do come in," he says softly.

Francie holds on to her son's hand. She has pinned her blonde curls up on both sides of her head with two combs whose red and black lacquer shines in the morning sunlight. The soft yellow shirt she wears pulled out over denim pants seems to float in the cool air. She is barefoot. A dream Marc thinks.

"Are you up, Marc?" She says. He can tell she wants to greet him in French. "You have *bien dormee?*"

"Yes, Francie, quite well." He smiles and cups the cigarette in his hand, the ash falling into his palm. "I didn't know you could speak French."

"A few years in high school. You know, Lycee. That's all I can remember."

"It is all right. I had three years in London during the, how do you say, the bombardment, the Blitz, to learn. They tell me I speak like a bloody proper Englishman." His grin tightens the scar under his lip that runs down into his neck, a clean white line against the grain of his beard.

"Did you sleep?" she stops as if she has remembered something, her mouth half open, the "well" silent. Marc looks out the window. He pushes against the memory of his own apartment, the one that he knows sits empty, his family missing.

"Oh, yes. Quite well. Like the dead," he pauses. "I can't tell you how good it felt after all these days at sea. No one can sleep on these births."

The little boy tugs at her hand and Francie looks over at Marc and says.

"This is Robbie. Say *bonjour* to Marc, Robbie. He's from France, you know. Where daddy was."

The boy, whose blue short pants and sandals match just like the saleswoman at Russek's promised they would, looks across the room. "Are you going to leave soon? My daddy's coming home tonight. Did you know that?"

Marc smiles, his face bright, his eyes sad. "I am very very happy to meet you, *Mon ami.* Very happy. You know how proud you have made you mama. She has told me you are the apple of her eye." He kneels down to look the boy in the eye, his fingers playing with the boy's tiny soft hands. "Your papa is a hero, you know. I am proud that I can stay with you, for few days. Perhaps we will have time to be friends, yes?"

As he stands, Marc finds Francie's face. A faint smudge just above her cheekbone points up at her green eyes framed by luxurious black lashes. "You are very gentle to allow me to stay here. It is all so new to me," he says, gesturing across the room, his head inclined to the French doors. "We can walk out there later, yes? Into the *parc, non?*"

"Yes. Perhaps we can take Robin out to ride his bike, yes." She stares back, her eyebrows arched in pleasure.

"Robin?"

"You know, Mr. Mark. Like the birdie. Its short for Robbie," the boy speaks with such seriousness that Francie covers her mouth to hide the smile that breaks across her face.

"Ah. *Monsieur Robin.* I understand. You are the harbinger of spring. You bring the end of winter. Did you know that?"

Robin twists from his mother's grasp, and screams "I know. I know. I know," and runs across the room. Francie starts to tell him to behave, but Marc bounds up behind the boy, scoops him gracefully up and places him on his shoulders. Together they walk over to the doors.

"There, *Monsieur Robin.* You can see all the way east, can you now? Where the sun comes up. Did you know that's where I have come from too? From the east?"

"Did you see, mom? Look how high I am. I can see all the way to the East. That's where Marc comes from." Robin pauses. "I thought you came from France."

Marc waits patiently in the downstairs living room that Francie "contributes" as his bedroom. After less than a week in this soft beige room he feels uneasy, off-balance. The room, adorned with oriental rugs, maple tables, and a light gray sofa that serves as his bed, has begun to replace his memory of the Quartier Latin where they had lived before. Before the German invasion. For the first time in four years he wills himself to awaken. But he cannot find l'esprit.

The Chagall oil over the sofa faces out toward the park, an invitation to enter through the two grand doors. One night Marc dreams that Chagall's dappled pony and the pale bride, her white veil floating over the rooftops, have come to scoop him up and return him to his family, back at *rue Monsieur Le Prince*. But when the horse flies by the window he sees nothing inside. The horse dissolves into an open car and Marc is driving, dressed his gray-green uniform, tall black boots pressing against the accelerator. Wermacht soldiers trudge along the side of the road salute him. He turns his head to see what the noise is about and looks at his family sitting behind him. They stare at him, uncomprehending. When he tries to speak he cannot. Words in English form in his brain, but he cannot make them into sounds. And then he is back on *rue Monsieur Le Prince* where all the rooms are empty, barren.

The clatter nineteen floors below, the muted honks and squeals that greet the war's end, rouse him. He is not in Paris, it is only where his dreams take him. He considers the word "transporter" but forces it out of his mind before it has time to ignite.

Francie tumbles the ice cubes into the glasses even before she hears him. "We like to start our weekends with a little pick-me-up. Scotch?"

She greets him, tray in hand, as he enters the room. The cut crystal decanter three quarters filled with honey-brown liquid balances two highball glasses jingling with ice. She wears a long black skirt and a white cotton top that she found in New Mexico. Beneath the turquoise necklace at her throat the coarse fabric of the blouse clings to the outline of her trim body. Her hair is loose and brushes her shoulders. Robin is nowhere in sight.

"Danny will be home in a few hours—if the train is on," she holds for a beat, "shed-u-el," softening the "k" like Myrna Loy. "He has another weekend furlough."

As Marc moves to the sofa Francie bends over to set the tray on the coffee table, sliding the silver cigarette lighter and case off to the side, glancing up at him, aware of the way he glances at her blouse. She kneels down, pours, her eyes never leaving his, and hands him the tall glass. "Oh, *pardon*," he says when he grasps the side of the glass, its condensation slippery and cold and then feels the warmth of her little finger. *"Pardon,"* he says again pulling his hand back. The tumbler rebounds against the front of his wrinkled white shirt, the stain now a dozen spots that spread in small dark circles across his chest. *"Zut,"* he exclaims, "now I have done it. It is clumsy of me." He slides the index finger of his free hand along the side of the glass, wiping the scotch up toward the rim of the glass. Then he laughs. "My first scotch since before the war. You must forgive me. It is such a wonder. All we had to drink in the Maquis was *vin rouge,* you know, red, spiked with Pernod when we could liberate it from the Boche."

Francie remains across the table from him, her black skirt clinging to her legs, her hands caressing the glass resting in front of her, her thumbs damp with moisture. This time when he lights a Gaulois, his closes his left eye against the spark of the match. He inserts the cigarette into the space between her fingers. The smoke curls above them as Francie puts her fingers to her mouth, takes a deep drag and passes it back to him.

"Salut," he looks deeply at her, feeling something stir.

"Doesn't anyone want to greet the hometown hero?" Dan leans his left shoulder, his long body sagging, into the doorway. "Got one for me, darling," he says in that Cary Grant voice Francie knows all too well.

It is almost a year since Francie opened the V-Mail with Danny's APO English address. "I'm ok, honey. Just a few wounds. I'm fortunate compared to many. My surgeon, a fellow from Brooklyn, tells me I'll be good as new. Kiss Robin for me." And now he is home. Almost. Weekend passes between rounds of "cutting" and "mending" of opening and then closing colostomy bags and putting the rod in and then taking it out of his left leg. "Good as new" means some things would never work the same. Almost a year since that letter from the hospital in England. She knew that he had been "in" on the Normandy landings—he quoted "Henry V" to her in May. She had held her breath, afraid to exhale.

Dan slouches in the doorway, his field coat tossed over his right shoulder. He jams his left hip and hand and cane against the frame for support. The army cap tilts off to one side, a mockery of how jaunty he looked when he enlisted. Small pale blue eyes look out from his strong-boned face with an intensity that seems to flare when the pain subsides. Fit and lanky once, now he looks weary and gaunt. The gold emblem of the 47th Infantry, the embossed eagle with lightning bolts in its talons, gleams from the side of his cap.

"And, Marc," he says, "Later you must tell me all about France. I only saw it from beneath a hedgerow, you know."

Francie hands him a highball, kisses him softly, and takes his jacket from his arm placing it across the back of a chair. She wonders if Marc sees his own reflection in the intimacy of her gesture. A sudden billow of wind from the park swirls through the room, inflating the coat's chest and sleeves and puffs out the array of ribbons and medals covering the left breast pocket. When the breeze subsides the coat settles back lifelessly against the skeletal outline of the chair.

Robin pulls the blanket over his head. The boy snuggles under the table in the hallway just outside the door to his parent's room. He loves his Indian blanket, cotton, with brown and pink and yellow designs woven into a New Mexico sunset. His uncle Nick, who watches for spies in Santa Fe, brought it to Robin on his last leave. It is Robin's favorite thing ever.

The long hall way is dark and Robin can almost hear, if he listens very hard, the sounds of night, the tiny crinkles that dance like faint gray dots in the air. The light from Marc's room at the other end of the hall barely peeks out from beneath the door. It isn't easy to reach his hand up over his forehead and tug the edge of the blanket down so that it reaches over his eyes just to the tip of his nose. But Robin wants to be invisible, to have just a tiny opening to breath from. The dark, square oak table fits him perfectly. The four legs are spaced wide enough to allow him to curl his body into a ball where he can wait for dawn. His father is about to leave for the hospital. He arrived on Friday night for two short days at home.

Robin visited him at the Army hospital in Fort Dix once. Francie took him on the train from Penn Station. The driver of the yellow De Soto cab had pulled down the leather jump seat so he could to sit facing backward. The train-ride had been bumpy and exciting. The car overflowed with soldiers and sailors in uniforms, their hands clutching the waists of girls with red ribbons in their hair, some drinking from large bottles so clear that Robin could see right through them. One soldier pulled a small black-green pineapple from his belt, began waving it around, and put the steel circle on the end into his teeth. The soldiers in the car erupted. One man grabbed Robin and pulled him down onto the floor of the train, pinning the boy's ear so that he could hear the staccato thumping and grinding of the steel wheels bursting in his head. A minute later it was over, the man with the grenade lay sleeping in the corner, his head cocked awkwardly against the metal door of the conductor's cabin.

When the crisply uniformed black conductor came by a few minutes later with his ticket punch clicking like a barber's scissor Francie let Robin hand over their tickets. "We're going to Fort Dix," the boy said, "to see my daddy." The conductor, the glossy brim of his cap pulled down to his eyes looked at Francie and winked. "You'll be wanting to get off at the next stop."

The hospital, long and wide, smelled of sweat and antiseptic and the sweet odor of a two dozen men. They lay in two rows of white enameled beds swathed in bandages, their eyes staring up at the bare white ceiling. A nurse led them down the center aisle and Robin searched each bed for his father's face. But except for an image that sat on Francie's dresser leaned up against the array of atomizers that reflected in the mirror, Robin could not actually remember him: only a name, Daniel, and a uniform with shiny buttons. No one in the hospital wore such a uniform, and some of the men had no faces.

Francie pulled them both between two beds, stepping over the metal feet of an IV stand, where she bent down to kiss the man whom they had come to see. He lay flat in his bed, one leg wrapped in a plaster-of-paris cast, white as snow, held suspended by a pulley. A small hospital table at his chin held a glass half filled with water, a straw bent so that he could drink without raising his head. When he started to speak Francie, her fingers twisted and white, interrupted, "Look who I brought to see you, dear," her voice cheerful, her eyes hard. Francie pulled Robin close, folding his face into her skirt.

Robin peered up at his father from below the edge of the bed as Dan reached his hand across his body to feel the boy's soft blonde hair touching it with the tips of his fingers.

"Isn't he just like his photographs, dear?" Her smile etched its lines into her face.

Dan's eyes yellow with pain and exhaustion met Robin's startled gaze. He started to speak, then stopped and reached back to the tray. He handed his son a small dog, constructed out of colored pipe cleaners, reds and blues and yellows, bent and twisted into shape.

"Oh, Dannie. This must be what you did in therapy." His mother's lipstick stuck to her front teeth.

The token felt like a scrub-brush, bristly and sharp. Robin held it and looked back at his father, remembering not to cry just like his mother had instructed. "Can we go home now," he said, not knowing why, as he took the multi-colored dog and pushed it into his pocket.

Robin huddles beneath the table, protected and hidden. He feels the dog scratch against the skin of his stomach where he has wedged it into the waistband of his flannel pajamas. The sounds coming from behind the door, the muffled chatter, the heavy footfall tell him that his father has awakened. He pulls the Indian blanket tighter over his face, slows his breathing, and closes his eyes, feigning sleep.

As the door clicks softly shut Robin dares to open one eye just enough to see his father's polished black shoe and smooth tan pants as he limps slowly down the hall. Robin watches his father, his left leg not bending, fused into the shape that the cast intended, his left hand pressing down hard on the handle of the cane. His father seems to step then halt, step then halt, his arm and shoulder rising and falling with the effort. Daniel stops, pauses, and reaches his hand out to touch Robin's door before he disappears around the corner. Moments later, Robin hears Francie stirring. She glides barefoot down the hall, her blonde hair flowing down her neck. She reaches out to open the door to Marc's room. Silently she enters.

    Dan convinced Francie to move into her mother's "grand" duplex apartment on Central Park West just after Pearl Harbor. Francie tried to refuse. She was horrified at what her Party friends would say. Bad enough they teased her about being a "premature fascist" for her "bourgeois taste." But, to her surprise Danny thought it a good idea. "Fuck the Party," he said, glancing up from the pile of law books that lay open on his desk. "There's a war on, no sense all that space going to waste." That was his way of telling her that he planned to enlist, do his duty for the cause, and for the as yet unborn baby. "I think it's a cockamamie idea," she said. But he laughed and tossed an eraser at her ass.
    "And you won't come down stairs unless we invite you?" Francie declared as her mother smiled.
    "Are you going to 11th Street today, dear." Her mother responded. Francie felt the sting. Her mother didn't smile this time.
    Downtown, on 11th Street, Francie always raised her hand first. Always. Later, when they told her that Marc Zitron had just arrived, she couldn't resist. A Frenchman, they said, a Russian Jew whose parents had come to Paris before the First War, with impeccable credentials: the French army, internment as a POW, the Resistance, and, of course, the Party. Post-war France found him too radical now, and there were some questions about his papers. They might never allow him back. And his family. A pity. All lost. Francie always gave them the money they asked for. Gladly said he could stay with them.
    "It's a bit of a mishmash, a *tsimmis,*" she said apologetically that

first night before showing him his room. "But you'll love the view of the park in the morning sun." She felt dizzy sitting next to him in the cab, excited by the feel of his arm against his when the cabbie swerved to avoid the red double-decker bus dawdling its way uptown.

Simmis?

"Yiddish. Mixed up, like a stew. "

His face brightens. "I know, everyone says I don't look Jewish either."

When she asks Marc what he does downtown he looks far away, "Oh, you know. Translation. That kind of thing. What ever they ask of me."

He tells her that Trachty, Alexander Trachtenberg, the publisher (and editor and copy editor and sole employee) of International Publishers has put him onto "important" documents. Stalin's recent diatribe against British Imperialism, "The Lion Reaches Across the Rhine," is his first week's assignment.

"Boring things mostly," he says. They are standing in the hallway. Dan has left for the hospital. She can feel Marc's body, palpable, in the air next to hers. They have the week together. She adores him and it scares her.

When Dan departs the next Monday he refuses to let Francie help him on with his uniform. She fears that he knows about Marc, and it makes her shiver. She bites the inside of her lower lip till she tastes blood. His weight pulls her body toward him as he sits on the edge of the bed. Now that the doctors have finished fusing his knee he has to learn to use the handle of his cane to hook under his belt and shimmy his pants up the length of his unbending leg. He sits struggling in the early dawn, the gray light giving way to a yellow glow across the park, while he sweats and struggles with the cane. He holds the cane's rubber tip in his fist. His right arm, the one bullets smashed into a circle of scar tissue as wide as a baseball, pulls it across his body. Francie cries silently as he stands and slips on his coat. The trickiest part is keeping his balance as he bends over to tie his shoe. The doctors at the hospital have warned her. He is afraid of pity, they say. It makes him feel even more helpless. She nodded as if she understood. Whenever she moves to hold him he looks away. "Try not to wake Robin," she says from the bed as he leaves. He turns in the door-way and smiles wanly. The light spills onto the carpet of their bedroom, and she sees the corner of Robin's Indian blanket peeking out from beneath the hall table just outside the door. Danny looks back at her, but his eyes are already elsewhere. Then he hobbles slowly down the hallway, glancing over his shoulder at his son feigning sleep under the table.

Francie and Marc walk behind Robin, who pedals his red tricycle furiously. His tiny legs pump up and down, his arms turn the handlebars to correct his wobbly path, then turn again. Robin swivels his head to make sure they are within eyeshot, then speeds ahead, stops and waits, searching out the park for stray squirrels and pigeons. The hexagonal paving stones clatter against the bike's tires. The racket tells Francie where Robin has gone when he disappears, momentarily, behind the bends that dip and curve along the way.

The spring sun tethered overhead warms Central Park's lush green and yellow fields. At the west edge of the park the El Dorado's art deco spires stab into the bright blue sky. "Is that where we live," Robin loves to ask, pointing at the open French doors, their curtains billowing inward in the breeze. "Is that my house?"

Marc stops at the Good Humor cart with a giant chocolate covered ice-cream bar painted onto its gleaming white side. "You would like an Eskimo?" he calls out to Francie.

"Eskimo?"

"Yes. Sure. You know. The ice cream on a stick. Eskimo's. Eskimo Pies we called them before the war. In the Luxembourg these man call out 'Eskimo!!' just when the children go home from school. My son always loved them. Maybe for Robin?"

But Robin has cycled out of their view and Francie worries that he has too many sweets in his diet. Dr. Dinkin had admonished her about the evils of sugar. "I didn't know you have a son," she said, and feels the mascara begin to blur along her lashes.

"I did. In Paris. A daughter too. It seems like a very long time ago." Francie half holds her breath, she waits, looks at Marc. Her longing is palpable. She wants him to tell her more.

"We …" he starts, and falters. "We …" he says again and then trails off.

Francie takes out a red calico bandana from her jeans, and wipes her eyes. "Oh, Marc. Not today. I don't want to ruin dinner." She fumbles with her back pocket, tucking the bandana behind her. "I don't know what to do." Her gold bracelet catches the light. It was all she wore the day they spent together in the beige room. She feels the first drops against the back of her neck.

"I don't either. I have no right. You. Us." Marc looks ahead. She can't tell if he knows that he's brushed the back of his hand against hers.

"Maybe if I knew about them it would help," she says softly, and turns her hand into his, feeling his tightness.

"I do not know what to tell you," he answers, "sometimes I forget where I am when we are together."

Within moments a storm pushes its way across the park. Wavering curtains of rain, sheer and fine, fill the air. Marc slips his coat around Francie's shoulders and guides her under the shelter of a tree. Robin has already beaten them to the patch of dark earth, where new shoots of yellow green grass have found temporary life in the spaces between the knobby roots of the tree spread above them.

"I feel so guilty. Can you help me, Marc?"

She knows he must feel her shiver under the pressure of his hand. Francie reaches down and pushes her son's curls back from his forehead, her fingers slick with the moisture that already coats his skin. The crack of lightning, the thunderclap that explodes above them less than a second later, fills the air with an electric glow. Marc's fingers stiffen and his body shivers. His hand grasps Francie's arm, and he gasps, a quick gulp of air that convulses him. His face is frozen, his eyes vacant.

"We should go back, should we?" He looks away, embarrassed. "I can't look him in the eye."

"I can't either. Let me give you up, Marc."

As they walk back across the park, Robin leading the way on his mud-splattered red cycle, Marc looks past Francie's eyes. "It felt like, you know, a bombardment. Like St. Lo. The Maquis sent me, my first time back to France in three years, I served as liaison between the Resistance and his army."

Francie sees him flinch, as if he wants to take his words back. But she wants to understand, to help him.

"I think Dan was there too. He won't talk about it. He was shot a week later. I never wanted him to go, you know."

Marc sighs. Around them the smell of the rain on the spring earth, of life.

"We never knew what hit us. The marking smoke, it was not where it was supposed to be. My unit, Maquis, we had dropped in the night before. We never even made contact with the *Amis*.

Even when I was on the train back from the POW camp in Germany in '41 it wasn't as bad at St. Lo. I don't think I will ever forget it. The mangled bodies, the smoke and fire. Terrible."

"The train?"

"Yes. When they sent us back from the prisons in Germany, the transports ..." his voice merging into silence.

His voice flattened. "When I came back to my apartment ... We lived on *rue Monsieur Le Prince* in the left bank. Near to the Sorbonne, you know. It was empty. When I see the furniture covered that way I knew they would never return. That was the day I left for London, for the Resistance. I have never returned."

Francie starts to speak. But Marc is already ahead of her, running silently toward Robin who is still pedaling and rocking, elbows and knees pumping. Extending his right arm out toward the boy, Marc places the flat of his palm against Robin's back and pushes the boy and the bike before him. Robin lifts his legs, stretching his feet out over the pedals, and raises his face to the sky. "Faster," he yells as he laughs, "Faster!"

"If we turn off the lights, you'll witness something spectacular, dear," Francie flicks the wall switch and crosses the room to open the doors and drapes wide. The red-blue glow of night outlines the silhouettes of the parade of buildings that line Fifth Avenue directly across the park. "It's our own private skyline," Francie says, "painted by Georgia O'Keeffe just for us."
Dan looks up at her from across the room. The window frames him. She can feel his eyes as they trace her, from the outline of curls cascading down the side of her face to her red toe-nails. "I thought O'Keeffe was thought to be decadent, hardly the art of the people," he says. "Not like our friend Marc," he motions to the canvas over her head, "another one of your dreamy Jewish socialists, isn't he."
Francie laughs. Her feels shrill, nervous. She lifts the highball takes a long pull, and swirls the ice around the inside of the glass. She gulps again, and goes still, her eyes blank, her hands knotted one into the other. "Mother says we're to come up for dinner later—the three of us. The maid will feed Robin down here."
"What does he do all day, this hero of the Resistance?"
Francie crosses the room and sits next to Dan, then reaches her hand out to hold his. "He says he was at St. Lo, too."
Dan sits staring at the warm glow from the window, not moving, his hand still and limp in hers.
"When you say St. Lo," his voice sounds dead, like the night, to her, "all I can see is the nozzle of the gun when it raked me. And that German soldier, just a boy." She waits for him to sob.
Down below the beefy doorman with rows of brass buttons parading up his chest whistles long and loudly for a cab.

Marc passes by the room and sees them sitting together. Now that Dan is home, "for good," as Francie says, his leg fused and the gaping hole in his shoulder healed, Marc is alone. He has no "papers," and as he told Francie, he has to be very careful. He takes different routes every day to the subway on his way down town. Sometimes he just walks all the way—straight down Broadway from Columbus Circle to Union Square. He can't stand the idea of being deported. There is no longer any place to go "home" to, he says, his eyes looking far out into the distance.

When Francie invites him to dine with them, he looks past her and says he is busy. She nods. He prefers wandering in the neighborhood, finding new places. Usually he goes into the Amsterdam Avenue A & P, a market where a white apron-ed grocery clerk armed with a long pole takes his order. "A can of tuna" the clerk repeats as he reaches the pole high to an unpainted wood shelf and squeezes. On the high end of the pole a u-shaped pincer clasps the tin, tipping it off the shelf, while the lower end the pole bears a handle to trigger the pincer. Marc marvels at the clerk's dexterity. He squeezes the handle with his lower hand, uses his upper to guide the pincer into place, and then topples the can into the folds of his apron in a single motion. The tuna with three slices of cheese and a small loaf of bread suffices for dinner.

"Thank you, Francie. I have plans," he says when she invites him again. He thinks about what he wants to say. About missing her. When he comes face to face with her in the hallway its as if he can't help himself. Then, she reaches out to touch his arm. "But Marc," she says, "you must wish for some company from time to time." He takes his eyes from hers and looks down.

"It is very difficult being here, you know. Your Dan he must need you even more, now" he finally speaks.

"He doesn't know what he needs," she looks at him again. She holds her breath. He can see the flecks of yellow on her iris. Sees her fingers twist the ring on her left hand.

"When they send us back from Germany, repatriation they called it, Petain agreed to send some Jews in France in return. The Vichy government sent my family with them. They took some boats down the Seine, loaded them at the quay behind Notre Dame, and, pff! they have disappeared. When I arrived home it was empty," he shrugs and lifts his eyebrows up. He thinks about reaching out to her, of folding her into his arms. But he cannot. Not again. "I only found out what finally happened to them when I come here."

Francie reaches her hand to his cheek, and kisses him delicately. "I'm so sorry Marc. So sorry." Then she turns and walks away. He follows her in his mind, but doesn't move.

For the next several weeks Marc sits in his room, smoking and looking out over the window. Sometimes he sits hunched up in the sofa, the bride and groom behind him blue-green in the evening light. At other times, especially mornings, he stands by the windows leaning out over the park, taking in the smells and sounds of the city coming to life. This perpetual spring-like moment, a daily new beginning, touches his senses. He comes to love the sounds and clatter of traffic, the squeals of tires on wet pavement and the grinding of the garbage trucks, the smell of dawn, and the glow of the sunrise, the bands of yellow and orange that reach across the park into his very room.

The door to Marc's room stands slightly ajar. Robin pushes tentatively against it, his hand barely at the level of the cut-glass knob that filters the morning light in green and gold. Robin walks silently to the sofa where Marc sleeps.

Robin watches Marc breathe. His lips are barely parted, his eyelids flutter like a moth's tiny wings. The boy reaches his hand, just the tips of his fingers, and places them on Marc's eyelids. Delicately, ever so delicately, he pushes the pad of his finger up, opening Marc's eye. Robin peers into the shimmering green orb, its tiny yellow and black lines radiating out from the deep surface just inches away.

Marc sees Robin's finger on one side of his nose, then he feels its pressure. The boy asks, "Are you sleeping?" with such sweetness that Marc must close his eyes to mask his tears. He smiles at the boy to shake the images that flicker to life.

Marc reaches his hand out to the boy and lifts him onto his chest. Robbie sits, his cotton-clad feet astride this stranger, and places his tiny hands around Marc's index fingers. "Are you still sleeping?" he asks.

Marc snores only just before he awakens. His wife once told him that; and he can feel the intake and shudder of his breath echo as he opens his eyes. The moment of waking takes him from peace to terror. It is almost four years since they disappeared and still the sense of loss remains like a throbbing pain, a phantom sensation like the nerves of severed limbs shooting into the brain. He can no longer clearly remember their faces—only their absence.

Suspended between sleep and wakefulness Marc less sees than senses the room, the open doors, the breeze, the boy now standing silently. Robin seems to float across the carpet, his blonde curls, tiny mouth, round cheeks faint in the early light. As Robin glides towards the windows, his small hands reaching out to catch the wind, Marc stirs, suddenly alert. The little boy turns to face the window. The rays of the morning sun bend around the boy, cast him in shadow, bathe the shape of his head in gold. Robin steps up over the doorway and reaches his hands out toward the black wrought-iron staffs that hold the railing. His left foot snags on the small metal tab in the floor that secures the door's closure and he pitches forward, the material of his light blue pajamas pulling down from his waist.

Even before Robin can reach his arms to brace himself against the black iron posts Marc screams, "Non" and snatches the boy, lifting him up in his arms. One arm reaches across Robin's back, the other cradles his legs. Robin wraps his arms around Marc's neck, and the two of them stand there, panting, grinning, and smiling.

They hold each other, looking out over the park, as Francie walks in to see what the noise is all about.

Peter, 1946—New York

Peter, 1959—New York

Clockwise, from top left—Harry, 1938; Peter, Central Park, 1943; Harry's NYC Board of Education ID and union card.

December 23, 1949

Dear Mr. and Mrs. Rutkoff,

We, who were Harry's colleagues and friends, ask to share one small part of your great sorrow.

We mourn his passing because we loved him for his warmth and his humanity, because he helped us and sustained us, because we admired his fearlessness and his hatred for all sham. Above all, by word and deed he fought for all of us, for all America, for a better world.

There is not one of us who did not seek his counsel, who did not delight in his conversation or marvel at the breadth of his wisdom and understanding.

His memory will not die among us.

Henry Abraham
Sandy Gaynes
Nathan K. Chandler
Edward R. Colleen
Emil Olivet

Ben and Kap'en
Max Weintraub
Sol Fisher
Eddie Katz
Maurice Rotskin

WAR DEPARTMENT
THE ADJUTANT GENERAL'S OFFICE
RECORDS ADMINISTRATION CENTER
4300 GOODFELLOW BOULEVARD
ST. LOUIS 20, MISSOURI

IN REPLY REFER TO:
AGRS-DA 201 Rutkoff, Harry
(6 Dec 47) 42 052 120

31 March 1948

SUBJECT: Letter Orders

TO: Mr. Harry Rutkoff
425 Riverside Drive
New York, New York

    1. By direction of the President, under the provisions of Executive Order 9419, 4 February 1944 (Sec. II, WD Bul. 3, 1944), a Bronze Star Medal is awarded for exemplary conduct in ground combat against the armed enemy to Private First Class (then Private) Harry Rutkoff, 42 052 120, 47th Infantry, on or about 16 July 1944 in the European Theater of Operations.

    2. Authority for this award is contained in Par. 15.1e AR 600-45 and is based upon General Orders No. 18, Headquarters 47th Infantry dated 1 August 1944.

    3. The Commanding Officer, Philadelphia Quartermaster Depot, will forward an engraved Bronze Star Medal direct to the recipient at the address shown above. This office will forward a Bronze Star Medal Certificate, under separate cover, direct to the recipient.

BY ORDER OF THE SECRETARY OF THE ARMY:

Alfred E. Bonniwell
Adjutant General

ENLISTED RECORD AND REPORT OF SEPARATION
HONORABLE DISCHARGE

1. LAST NAME - FIRST NAME - MIDDLE INITIAL	2. ARMY SERIAL NO.	3. GRADE	4. ARM OR SERVICE	5. COMPONENT
Rutkoff Harry None	42 052 120	Pfc	Inf	AUS

6. ORGANIZATION	7. DATE OF SEPARATION	8. PLACE OF SEPARATION
Company "K" 47th Infantry	17 Jan 46	Tilton Gen Hosp Fort Dix NJ

9. PERMANENT ADDRESS FOR MAILING PURPOSES	10. DATE OF BIRTH	11. PLACE OF BIRTH
300 Central Park West New York	25 Jul 10	New York New York

12. ADDRESS FROM WHICH EMPLOYMENT WILL BE SOUGHT	13. COLOR EYES	14. COLOR HAIR	15. HEIGHT	16. WEIGHT	17. NO. DEPEND.
Same as item 9	Blue	Brown	6'1¼"	182 lbs.	2

18. RACE	19. MARITAL STATUS	20. U.S. CITIZEN	21. CIVILIAN OCCUPATION AND NO.
WHITE X	MARRIED X	YES X	Teacher, H.S. 0-31.01

MILITARY HISTORY

22. DATE OF INDUCTION	23. DATE OF ENLISTMENT	24. DATE OF ENTRY INTO ACTIVE SERVICE	25. PLACE OF ENTRY INTO SERVICE
5 Nov 43		26 Nov 43	New York New York

26. SELECTIVE SERVICE DATA	26. REGISTERED	27. LOCAL S.S. BOARD NO.	28. COUNTY AND STATE	29. HOME ADDRESS AT TIME OF ENTRY INTO SERVICE
X	YES X NO	#12	New York New York	139 W 82nd St New York New York

30. MILITARY OCCUPATIONAL SPECIALTY AND NO.	31. MILITARY QUALIFICATION AND DATE
Rifleman 745	Rifle Marksman Combat Infantryman's Badge

32. BATTLES AND CAMPAIGNS
Normandy GO 33 WD 45   Northern France GO 33 WD 45

33. DECORATIONS AND CITATIONS Two Bronze Battle Stars
American Theater Ribbon   Victory Ribbon
European African Middle Eastern Theater Ribbon   Purple Heart

34. WOUNDS RECEIVED IN ACTION
European Theater   7 Aug 44

35. LATEST IMMUNIZATION DATES

SMALLPOX	TYPHOID	TETANUS	OTHER (specify) Typhus
27 Nov 42	18 Dec 43	5 Feb 44	16 May 44

36. SERVICE OUTSIDE CONTINENTAL U.S. AND RETURN

DATE OF DEPARTURE	DESTINATION	DATE OF ARRIVAL
12 May 44	E A M E Theater	27 May 44
25 Sep 44	United States	9 Oct 44

37. TOTAL LENGTH OF SERVICE

CONTINENTAL SERVICE			FOREIGN SERVICE		
YEARS	MONTHS	DAYS	YEARS	MONTHS	DAYS
1	9	16	0	4	27

38. HIGHEST GRADE HELD Private First Class

39. PRIOR SERVICE None

40. REASON AND AUTHORITY FOR SEPARATION
Certificate of Disability for Discharge Sec I AR 615-361 4 Nov 44 & 1st Indorsement Tilton General Hospital Fort Dix New Jersey 15 Jan 46

41. SERVICE SCHOOLS ATTENDED None

42. EDUCATION (Years)

Grammar	High School	College
8	4	4

PAY DATA

43. LONGEVITY FOR PAY PURPOSES			44. MUSTERING OUT PAY		45. SOLDIER DEPOSITS	46. TRAVEL PAY	47. TOTAL AMOUNT, NAME OF DISBURSING OFFICER
YEARS	MONTHS	DAYS	TOTAL	THIS PAYMENT			
2	2	13	$300.00	$100.00	None	$39.5	$118.21 J L WILLIAMS CAPT FD a/o DONALD A LA FACE MAJ FD

INSURANCE NOTICE

IMPORTANT IF PREMIUM IS NOT PAID WHEN DUE OR WITHIN THIRTY-ONE DAYS THEREAFTER, INSURANCE WILL LAPSE. MAKE CHECKS OR MONEY ORDERS PAYABLE TO THE TREASURER OF THE U.S. AND FORWARD TO COLLECTIONS SUBDIVISION, VETERANS ADMINISTRATION, WASHINGTON 25, D.C.

48. KIND OF INSURANCE	49. HOW PAID	50. Effective Date of Allotment Discontinuance	51. Date of Next Premium Due (One month after 50)	52. PREMIUM DUE EACH MONTH	53. INTENTION OF VETERAN TO
Nat. Serv. X U.S. Govt. None	Allotment X Direct to V.A.	31 Dec 45	31 Jan 46	$7.40	Continue Continue Only Discontinue X

55. REMARKS (This space for completion of above items or entry of other items specified in W.D. Directives)
Lapel Button and Patch Issued
ASR Score (2 Sep 1945) - 54
Enlisted Reserve Corps 5 Nov 43 to 25 Nov 43

54. RIGHT THUMB PRINT

56. SIGNATURE OF PERSON BEING SEPARATED
Harry Rutkoff

57. PERSONNEL OFFICER (Type name, grade and organization - signature)
A. ANDERSON 2ND LT MAC
ASST PERSONNEL OFFICER

WD AGO FORM 53-55
1 November 1944

This form supersedes all previous editions of WD AGO Forms 53 and 55 for enlisted persons entitled to an Honorable Discharge, which will not be used after receipt of this revision.

BOARD OF EDUCATION OF THE CITY OF NEW YORK

SAMUEL GOMPERS VOCATIONAL and TECHNICAL HIGH SCHOOL

455 SOUTHERN BOULEVARD at 145th STREET, NEW YORK 55, N. Y.

MOTT HAVEN 5-0950 -0951

EDWARD N. WALLEN, Principal   DEPARTMENT

May 14, 1951

Mr. and Mrs. Simon Rutkoff
865 Walton Avenue
New York, N.Y.

Dear Mr. and Mrs. Rutkoff :

    As a tribute to the memory of your son and our esteemed colleague, Harry Rutkoff, members of the faculty of the Samuel Gompers Vocational and Technical High School have set up a fund for an annual medal to be awarded in his name at each graduation exercise. This medal is awarded to the member of the graduation class who has the highest average in Social Studies, and who is of good character.

    The members of the Social Studies Department, who, as a group, initiated the tribute to a departed friend and colleague, voted that the first two medals to be struck be presented to the parents and the widow of the deceased.

    I am, therefore, herewith presenting you with the enclosed medal as a measure of our respect and feeling for a man we knew. Our principal, Mr. Edward N. Wallen, has asked me to convey his own respects also.

                               Sincerely,

                                 Sanford J. Gaynes
                                 Chairman, Rutkoff Memorial
                                    Award Committee

About The Authors

Harry Rutkoff taught in the New York City public school system before going off to war in 1943. He was wounded in France and never recovered from his wounds. Harry died in 1949.

Peter Rutkoff has been teaching at Kenyon College in Ohio since 1971. From 1999-2001, Peter held the National Endowment for the Humanities Distinguished teaching chair at Kenyon. His other books include *New York Modern: The Arts and the City* with William B. Scott (Johns Hopkins University Press, 2001), *Shadow Ball: A Novel of Baseball and Chicago,* (McFarland, 2001) and *Cooperstown Chronicles: Camp and Other Love Stories,* Birch Brook Press, 2002.